MEET DOCTOR HALL

A Young Woman Searches for Her Truth

BY
PATRICIA BAILEY

Copyright © 2023 Patricia Bailey

MEET DOCTOR HALL : A Young Woman Searches for Her Truth

Quantity sales special discounts are available on quantity purchases by corporations, associations, and others. For details, contact the publisher at carol@markvictorhansenlibrary.com

Orders by U.S. trade bookstores and wholesalers.
Email: carol@markvictorhansenlibrary.com

Creative Contributor - Veronica "Ronni" Deisler
Photography - Paul Bartell - Paul@ProPhotoGraphics.com
Cover Design & Book Layout - DBree, StoneBear Design

Manufactured and printed in the United States of America distributed globally by markvictorhansenlibrary.com

MVHL

New York | Los Angeles | London | Sydney

ISBN: 979-8-88581-080-7 Hardback
ISBN: 979-8-88581-081-4 Paperback
ISBN: 979-8-88581-082-1 eBook
Library of Congress Control Number: 2022922718

DEDICATION

For
Garrison

Contents

Introduction

A few years after we were married, Garrison received word that his Aunt Susie had passed away, and he was to inherit the home his grandfather, Dr. Hall, had built in Washington State.

When we arrived there, it was clear that it was not your average house. Garrison was an architect and pleased that his grandfather had hired an architect to design the home. The Asian influence was evident from the beautiful wooden arched gateway into the property. There was one path that divided into two with a lily pond between them. One path led to the residence and the other to Dr. Hall's office.

The house was warm and inviting with a large stone fireplace in the center of the living room, real fir wood floors and walls. Every wall was decorated with Chinese tapestries, framed embroideries or paintings, and the hallways were lined with books. Elegant vases and bowls in Chinese patterns were scattered about.

However, the real treasures were in the lower-level basement of the home. There we found four large trunks that Dr. Hall had brought back from China. We were thrilled and delighted when we opened each one to find them full of exquisite, embroidered robes, tapestries and collections of Qing (late 1800s) dynasty items. I had never seen such beautiful things! It certainly sparked what became my lifelong interest and appreciation of Chinese art.

The third trunk we opened was full of Dr. Hall's handwritten journals of his time in China, which are presented in this book. It was not common for an American missionary Doctor to be in China during that time and he offered a rare glimpse of life in that time and place. The stories were incredible! Dr. Hall was a gifted writer and poet, and he wrote of his daily experiences in a totally foreign land with insight, empathy, wisdom and great humor. He writes of his journey down the Yangtze River where he was almost captured by river pirates. Another time, he was fed to wild dogs and other spellbinding stories. Many of his stories were published in *Asia, The American Magazine on the Orient*.

I have tried to present a small portion of his prolific writings in this book. It is my hope that the reader will be transported, as I was, to another time and place with a greater appreciation of all cultures. It was Dr. Hall's true desire to elevate, help and love other human beings—that they would realize the love that God has for all.

On the next page, you will see the painting I was inspired to create from the original photograph, as seen on the cover.

1

MEETING
LAO LAO

Grace Bennett stood at the San Francisco Airport arrivals curb with her luggage, waiting in line for a taxi. There were several people in front of her. Not that she was in a hurry. She'd caught an early morning flight from Newark Airport and was tired, but not looking forward to this visit. What little she knew about her mother's mother only made her more anxious.

Until now, Grace's relationship with her grandmother had amounted to the red envelopes with money she'd received every birthday growing up. The envelopes had also arrived at Chinese New Year, an occasion which her Chinese mother never acknowledged. Once, when she was a child, her mother had taken her to visit her grandmother in San Francisco. Grace recalled a tall, dark-haired, stern-looking woman who refused to hug her when she reached up. "We don't believe in hugs," the woman had said. "Ask your mother." Grace had looked up at Julie, who was biting her lips. It had been the first sign that her mom and grandmother didn't get along.

At that moment, the next taxi driver waved her over. Me? She pointed to herself with confusion. Still ahead of her was a well-dressed Chinese couple with a sleepy little girl, resting her head on her father's shoulder. Grace deferred to the family in front of her, but the driver jumped out, grabbed her suitcase, and tossed it into the trunk of his cab, growling,

"C'mon, girlie. I don't have all day." Confused, she hopped into the back seat. "Can't stand those Chinks," the driver said as he returned to the car. "Won't pick 'em up if I don't have to. Where to, miss?"

Grace shuddered when she heard the offensive ethnic slur. She glanced out of the car window at the Chinese couple, who stared back without expression. It wasn't the first time this had happened to them, she guessed. Prejudice was something she'd encountered before, but not personally. She'd inherited her mother's straight black hair, but not her almond-shaped eyes, smaller nose, and wide cheekbones. Instead, she was born with her English father's oval face, pale complexion, and well-shaped larger nose. As a result, she'd misled others in the past. People were surprised to learn that her mother was Chinese—that is, the few who'd met her mother. She felt uncomfortable now, passing at the expense of the Chinese couple, but it gave her satisfaction to know she was fooling the taxi driver.

She leaned forward to give the driver her grandmother's address in Berkeley, then sat back as the cab lurched away from the curb. Her cell phone rang. It was her mother, Julie.

"Hi, Mom."

"You could have called when you arrived," her mother said. "I had to find out by checking arrivals online."

"Sorry. I forgot."

"Did you get to your grandmother's yet?"

"Not yet. I'm in a taxi on the way," Grace answered.

"Don't forget what I told you about your shoes. You need to take them off when you step into her house. It's the Chinese way." Her mother's voice was firm. "She'll probably have some slippers or something for you to put on inside."

"You've told me that a hundred times, Mom."

"And don't call her 'Grandma' the way you did with your father's mother. You need to call her 'Lao Lao.' Now say it back to me."

"I know how to say it, Mom. I'm 21. I'm in college. Remember?"

"I remember, Grace. I just don't want you to get off on the wrong foot with her. She can be difficult," her mother said.

"If she's so difficult, why couldn't *you* come to help pack up her house? You're her daughter," Grace whined.

After a long pause, her mother sighed and said, "We've been through this, Grace. She wants to come live with me. All Chinese parents expect their children to take care of them when they get old. But it would never work with us. She's too Chinese and I'm too . . . American, I guess. We'd be at each other's throats. Besides, I'm overloaded with work right now. Having you help her move to a senior citizen complex is my way of compromising."

"Oh, great," Grace replied. "I get to be *your* compromise."

"I really appreciate your doing this for me, sweetheart." Her mother's voice softened. "You know, it's good for you to learn a little about the culture we came from. Goodness knows, I haven't taught you much about it."

"Yeah, I'm dying to learn more about being Chinese, so I can pretend even harder that I'm not." Grace rolled her eyes. She checked to see if the cab driver had heard her, but he was humming a tune.

"Stop rolling your eyes, Grace," her mother said. "If my father hadn't died so young, I would have loved to learn more from him. But your grandmother . . . never mind. Look, it's only for a few weeks. Once she's settled, you'll be back with your friends here for the rest of the summer. Uh-oh, I gotta go, Hon. Give my best to your grandmother—I mean your 'Lao Lao.' Love you."

Grace didn't understand why her mother suddenly wanted her to learn about her Chinese heritage after all these years of ignoring it. Whenever Grace had asked about it, her mother had waved her away. After a while, she stopped asking. As she grew older, she saw how negative some people were toward anyone who was Asian American. Some children in her class at school weren't allowed to play with Grace. When she broke down and cried, because she hadn't been invited to a birthday party, she asked her mother why. "Some folks avoid people who don't look or sound like them," her mother explained. When Grace protested she couldn't see a difference between her and the other girls at school, her mother had sighed. "Their parents have met me, Grace. They can see I'm Chinese. I suspect it's because of me they did not invite you."

Before Grace started college at New York University, her mother sat her down and revealed some of the discrimination she'd experienced: ethnic slurs, racial jokes, threats. She'd never walked alone at night for fear that someone might attack her because of what she looked like. Some Asians had been beaten and even killed because of their appearance. "You're fortunate, Grace, that you look like your father and not me," she said. "Take advantage of that. Be careful to share your ethnic background only with people you can trust."

Grace took her mother at her word. The only one who knew the truth was her roommate, Samantha, a light-skinned Jamaican American, who had her own issues with passing. Grace and Sam had hit it off from the start. It wasn't long before they were sharing all their secrets and concerns with each other. But lately, Sam began hiding more than her ethnic background. During their junior year, Grace noticed her friend's drug use, and now she was worried Sam was in over her head.

"It's no biggie," Sam said, when Grace confronted her. "I need something to help me stay awake so I can get my homework done. Then I need to take something else so I can sleep," she laughed. "C'mon, Gracie. You know how my family is about grades. Same as yours." She laughed again. "Besides everybody does it, and it'll be all over when I graduate Summa Cum Laude."

Grace understood. Her mother wasn't exactly a "tiger mom," but she was adamant about her grades. Fortunately, Grace never had trouble keeping up. She was a good test taker. It ran in the family. Her mom had received a PhD in psychology and had her own private practice. Her father, who passed away three years ago, had been a well-respected cardiologist. From an early age, he'd encouraged Grace to pursue medicine as a career. Now that she was approaching her senior year of college, it was time for her to make a decision. She had mixed feelings, though. Her favorite classes had been her electives in writing. She'd always loved to write, since she was a child. And she was good at it. It was never work for her. Still, she knew a career in writing wasn't practical. But medical school would be both difficult and time-consuming, and it wouldn't give her much time to enjoy other pursuits. She'd loved her parents, but they both seemed to be more dedicated to their careers than to raising her. She wanted a different kind of life.

Just then, Grace heard a beep and noticed it was a text from her boyfriend, Adam.

"Are you there yet? Miss you," Adam texted.

"Yeah. Miss you, too. I'm in a cab on my way to my grandmother's house." She texted back. Adam didn't know that her grandmother was Chinese . . . or her, for that matter. They'd been dating for only three months, and she wasn't sure how he'd react, so she hadn't told him. If he asked, she'd tell him the truth, of course. Not that he would know to ask. She put that thought in the back of her mind for now.

"Going to the Jersey Shore next week," Adam texted.

Grace answered, "Have fun. Wish I could go, too." This trip was ruining her summer vacation. She'd made plans with several of her girlfriends and now she was missing out.

Adam responded, "Glad you're ok. TTYL.

"Yeah, TTYL." She was happy Adam had texted her but frustrated that he was so abrupt. Even on the phone, he wasn't particularly chatty. A little more than "miss you" would have been nice. Even an emoji heart would have been something.

"We're here, miss," the driver spoke for the first time in an hour. "I'll get your suitcase out of the trunk."

Grace paid the driver and gave him a modest tip. She

couldn't justify being too generous, after the racist comment he'd made before they took off.

"Yeah . . . thanks," he said, with little enthusiasm.

Grace watched as he drove away, then turned to examine her grandmother's house. It was a pale-yellow, bungalow-style house with stucco siding and a small front yard. She recalled, from her college elective in architecture styles, that bungalows were built during the early 1900s, so it was probably pretty old. An exotic assortment of flowers and shrubs were planted, in an orderly fashion, on both sides of the yard. It was the only sign that an Asian woman might live here, she thought. There was a craftsman-style picture window on the right side of the house, a sheer, white curtain partly concealing the view of the interior. To the left were five concrete front steps, with wrought-iron railings, leading up to a small wraparound porch. The house didn't appear large from the front, but Grace could see that it extended far back, probably because of an addition long ago.

Grace picked up her suitcase and walked up the front steps to the house. The gray front door had a small window with four panes and there were two narrow, vertical windows, one on either side of the door. The windows, which were covered with the same sheer, white curtains as the front window, had a similar wooden craftsman-style design at the top. Grace took a deep breath and rang the doorbell. She heard a shuffle of feet, and the curtain on the right-side window was pulled back. A face, similar to her mother's, but lined with wrinkles and brown spots, peered out. She heard a series of locks un-click, one by one, and the door opened at last. Steel gray hair, pulled back in a bun, framed the old woman's wizened face, and she wore loose-fitting, long, blue pants and a multi-colored over-blouse with a mandarin collar. She was a little under five feet tall, Grace guessed. So much for her memories, she thought as she looked down at the 84-year-old woman from her height of five-six.

"Hello, Lao Lao," Grace said. "I'm your granddaughter, Grace."

2

Who is Dr. Hall?

race's grandmother, Lao Lao, looked her up and down, then turned her around. "Hmph," she grunted. "You still look like your father. Too bad," she said, shaking her head in disappointment. "Your hair is dark. Good. You should let it grow long. That's the style with young people today. At least you look healthy and strong. I guess Julie did something right." Her grandmother turned back into the house. "What are you waiting for? Come in. I have something to show you," she said. "Leave your shoes by the door. You will find a few slippers. One should fit you."

Grace stepped inside the house and dropped her suitcase with a thud.

"Not so loud," her grandmother said in a shrill, high-pitched voice. "You'll wake up the spirits."

Not as much as your voice, Grace thought. She removed her shoes and laid them on a mat by the door, next to a smaller pair of shoes. Surprised to see such an assortment of slippers, she chose the largest pair and squeezed her feet into them. It looked as if her grandmother had a lot of visitors.

She grabbed her suitcase and followed her grandmother down a long hallway that was wallpapered with blue flamingos, blue bird cages, and blue flowers on a white background. Grace felt like she was walking through a strange, blue world. As she glanced to her right, she saw a living room, furnished with a deep-blue sofa and a glossy, black-lacquered coffee table that stood on a thick Chinese rug. She stepped in to get a closer look, and her grandmother let out what sounded like an impatient sigh at the entrance to the room. "Your ye ye—that is, your grandfather—and I owned a gift store in San Francisco's Chinatown when we were young," she explained. "After he died, I sold the store, but I couldn't part with some of the furniture and gifts. Everything you see here is from our store."

Grace studied the delicate scene painted on the coffee table's surface, then ran her palm over one of the striking, hand-carved legs, featuring a lion's head at one end and a claw foot at the other. Behind her, two matching black-lacquered end tables sat next to a couple of accent chairs. "These are so beautiful," she whispered.

"They're Ming armchairs," her grandmother's eyes gleamed with pride. "Lacquer is an ancient Chinese technique. It comes from the sap of a special tree in China, then is mixed with chemicals to create different colors. A black lacquer was applied to the hand-carved arms and backs of these chairs. The seats are upholstered with fine red and gold silk. Your Ye Ye came from a well-to-do Chinese family. His father imported many antiques and quality pieces for the store, before his son and I took over."

Grace noticed that the rug had a blue border and a black interior with intricate flowers woven into it, and it matched the room's other furnishings. On the inside wall of the room, was a large, rectangular mirror, framed in black-lacquered wood. It had a simple Chinese mountain scene painted on it.

Her grandmother sounded like the saleswoman she once was. "As you can see, I finished the wood cabinet below the mirror with red lacquer and a hand-painted Chinese landscape. The blue and white vase, with the round bottom, that sits on top, is a porcelain ball vase. This one has a dragon painted on it. And that," she pointed to the enormous, black-lacquered screen that stood behind the couch and filled the entire width of the room with its ten panels, "is my favorite. The scene painted on the screen reminds me of my old home in China."

"It's incredible," Grace murmured. "I had no idea Chinese furniture could be so beautiful. It looks like it's new."

Her grandmother grunted, "That's because we never use it," she said in a matter-of-fact voice. "Come. We're wasting time. I have something more important to show you."

They continued down the hallway until they reached two doors, one on either side. To the left, Grace glimpsed a serviceable-looking kitchen with a small Formica table and two chairs, but to the right was another surprise. "Ai, I guess you must see my dining room, also," said her grandmother. Grace walked in and nearly collided with one of eight chairs that surrounded an enormous, round, dark-wood table that filled the room. She wasn't sure there was enough space to walk around it. "In China, the family likes to eat together," Lao Lao continued her lesson. "We enjoy each other's company with a round table because it's easier to share. This table is made from dark cherry rosewood. In the middle is a smaller, revolving table. It's what Americans call a 'Lazy Susan,' but it was invented by the Chinese many centuries ago. We place our food in the middle, and we can turn it so everyone can choose what they want without having to pass it."

Grace noticed the outer edge of the table was hand-carved, as were the backs of the chairs. The seat covers featured beige dragons on an olive-green floral design. *Dragons seemed to be a popular theme in China*, she thought.

"As you can see," her grandmother went on, "my China cabinet is made from the same wood."

Grace looked at the cabinet, which was a tight fit in the corner of the room. Admiring the hand-carved flower and bird design, she noticed there were some figurines inside.

"These are my favorite porcelain and jade statues," her grandmother said as she opened the glass doors of the cabinet and picked up a jade dragon from one of the shelves. "This was Julie's favorite when she was young. I'm surprised she didn't take it when she left."

Grace heard the bitterness in her voice. "Yeah, well—" She didn't want to get into a debate about her mother's relationship with her grandmother. "So, where do I sleep?" she asked, changing the subject.

Her grandmother led her down the hallway that seemed never to end.

"You will sleep in this room," her grandmother said. "It's where my māma and bába slept while they lived with me. We didn't have bedroom furniture at our store, so I had to furnish it simply. I think they liked it that way. It reminded them of the simpler life they had back in China."

Grace placed her suitcase beside the bed and examined the room. It was not as ornate as the others, but it still had a Chinese feel. There was a full-size platform bed with a headboard but no footboard. A large white, paper shade with painted green leaves on slender trees hung on the wall behind it. Several black and white photos were placed throughout the room. The his-and-hers dressers looked to Grace like the kind you'd find in IKEA today. There was a small table on either side of the bed, each holding a porcelain lamp with a blue and white design, similar to the ball vase in the living room. Next to one small table was a chair with a green and gold cushion and a rounded back. Unlike the other rooms, the wood in this one had a light tone and gave it a fresh appearance. Grace was surprised that her grandmother had such modern taste for an old woman. She tested the chair and was delighted to find it so comfortable.

"It's called a Monk chair. It was where my bába sat when he was tired."

Grace watched as her grandmother's face softened at the memory. But not for long.

Ha!" she said, "He was tired so often, I worried he might wear a hole in it." Her grandmother pointed to a door on her left. "You have your own bathroom, Grace. Do you like the room?"

"Yes, very much," Grace answered. "It feels so light and airy in here."

"That is because all this furniture is made from bamboo," her grandmother said with a satisfied smile, "which grows in China. Bamboo is strong and will last a very long time. It's a good substitute for wood because it resists insects and moisture and grows quickly. It's what they call 'eco-friendly' here. Ha! I sound like a television commercial."

Grace smiled back. Despite her grandmother's abruptness, she seemed to have a sense of humor.

"And now I will show you what I found this morning." her grandmother said. "I wanted to show you earlier, but you seemed more interested in a tour of my house first," she complained. "Come with me." Bristling with excitement now, she shuffled down the hall, leading Grace to another bedroom, similar to the first. "This is where I sleep." She indicated a small room off her bedroom. "It is also where I keep my precious storage."

Grace followed her grandmother into the added room, which was jam-packed with an assortment of Chinese artifacts and antiques on shelves against the wall. She began to examine one.

"No, no," her grandmother said, once again abrupt. "Those are important, yes, but this is what I want you to see." She gestured toward an old wood trunk, sitting among other boxes and trunks in the tiny room. It had an elaborate brass opener and mysterious, Chinese symbols carved in leather on the front. Grace noticed that the top and side were scratched and scuffed, and it didn't seem to be as valuable as the other antiques. "Open it," her grandmother demanded.

When she lifted the lid and looked inside, Grace was confused. It seemed to be filled with old, faded, sepia photographs and papers, some typed and some handwritten, as well as worn leather covers embossed with initials. These appeared to be journals, but were so old and worn, the handwritten pages were slipping out. She looked up at Lao Lao. "I don't understand. What's this?" she asked.

"They are the photographs and writings of Dr. William L. Hall, a medical missionary who traveled from the United States to the Shansi Province of China in 1896," her grandmother announced. "That's all I know. They've been stored here, untouched for decades. My mother told me that Dr. Hall gave his papers to your great-great grandmother for safekeeping before he returned home in 1922. She gave the trunk to my parents who brought it over to the States when we came after the war in 1945. They wanted to find Dr. Hall when they arrived, but they spoke little English and didn't know how to go about it. I was only seven."

"Why would he give his papers to my great-great grandmother?"

Lao Lao shook her head, as if disappointed in Grace's lack of understanding. "The women in our family may have been poor in the past, but we've always been forward thinking. She was one of the first women to be trained as a nurse in China. My lao lao told me she eventually worked with Dr. Hall and became a trusted friend."

"Okay, but why are they so important to you?" Grace asked.

"They're part of our history, Grace. I want to pass it on to others so they can understand what life was like in China during the late 1800s and early 1900s. How the people thought and acted. Aren't you curious?"

"I guess so," Grace said, but she wasn't sure. She had mixed feelings about her Chinese heritage. "Doesn't it make more sense to donate them to a museum, or something? I mean, you have to make a big move in a month. Your furniture will never fit into a couple of rooms in a senior complex. Wouldn't it be better to spend our time figuring out where everything will go? I'm sure a museum would be happy to take some of your antique pieces. Maybe you could give the rest away to friends and even sell a few on consignment. I'd be glad to help with that."

"No!" her grandmother shouted. "Dr. Hall entrusted this to my grandmother, and she has entrusted it to us. It's our familial duty to study these papers and make them known to the world. He may no longer be alive, but I'm sure his family would be happy to learn about his work. There are more opportunities today to find someone who is related to him. We must do what we can."

Grace realized how stubborn her grandmother could be. "Okay, okay. I didn't mean to upset you," she said. "But if Dr. Hall's papers are so important, why didn't you try to find him before? You've been living here since my mother was a kid."

Grace was surprised when her grandmother looked down at her feet. "I'm ashamed to tell you I only opened this trunk today. I expected to find some clothing or household goods. Nothing significant. I didn't realize how important his papers were. I'm not sure that my parents understood either, since they didn't speak or read English well. But now that I know, I must do something about them. And you must help me, Grace." Lao Lao was adamant.

Grace sighed. Her visit was getting more complicated. She

wondered if she'd get a chance to enjoy the Jersey Shore this summer at all. Meanwhile, she was hungry and tired from her trip. What was her grandmother planning for dinner anyway? She'd had Chinese food before, but her mom said that real Chinese food was different. Grace was wondering whether she'd like "real" Chinese food when her grandmother read her thoughts.

"Ai, where are my manners? You must be hungry. Did you eat on the plane? Never mind. I made something for us. Why don't you put away your clothes, Grace? You can use either dresser. There's plenty of room. I'll call when supper is ready."

With that, she disappeared, and Grace made her way back to her room. The first thing she lifted out of her suitcase was a new notebook she'd bought for this trip. Back home, she had over a dozen thick notebooks, filled with stories and essays she'd written. She hoped she would find something to write about while she was here. She left the notebook on top of a dresser, and after putting her clothes away, she gave her mom a quick call.

"Are you there?" Julie asked.

"Yes, Mom. It's . . . uh . . . not what I expected. The living room is something else, with all that Chinese furniture. It's beautiful."

"That's because we were never allowed to use it," her mom laughed.

"I don't know where she's going to put all her stuff when she moves. But she seems more interested in this trunk she discovered today."

"What trunk?"

"I don't know. It's an old beat-up trunk that used to belong to some doctor who went to China over a hundred years ago. She wants me to read his journals and figure out how to get it to his family," Grace answered.

"I don't remember a trunk. Where did it come from?"

"She says her parents brought it over when they moved here," Grace said. "One of my "great greats" was a nurse or something who knew the doctor. His name is Hill or Hall; I don't remember. He gave the trunk to her for safekeeping. Why he didn't take it home with him, I don't know. Anyway, Lao Lao went on and on about how it was our family responsibility to do something. She wants me to read all his papers, which is gonna take forever, Mom. You said I only had to stay a couple of weeks," Grace whined. "At this rate, I'll be here all summer!"

"Don't worry, sweetheart. She gets on these crazy kicks sometimes. I'm sure she'll forget about it in a day or two."

"Grace!" It was her grandmother yelling from the kitchen. "Supper is ready!"

"Gotta go, Mom," Grace said. "Lao Lao is calling me. Bye."

Grace wasn't sure if they were eating at the big table in the dining room or in the kitchen. She was relieved to learn it was the latter. The furniture in the kitchen looked like a well-kept relic from the 1950s. Her grandmother had set a small, red, Formica table with two, blue, ceramic bowls of soup, white paper napkins, a bamboo basket covered with a yellow cloth, and a long, green, plastic, serving dish filled with chicken dumplings. Grace sat in one of the two matching red vinyl chairs. The walls were painted white, and the cabinets were a pastel green. *All in all, it was a colorful scene*, she thought.

"It's noodle soup," her grandmother said. "I don't know what your mother makes for you, so I will introduce you to Chinese cuisine little by little. You can eat these with it." She removed the cover from the bamboo basket which was filled with steamed buns.

"Noodle soup sounds good," Grace said. She started to eat but was embarrassed to hear her grandmother slurping the soup from her spoon. She looked up at her.

"You don't like your soup, Grace?"

"It's delicious, Lao Lao. What makes you think I don't like it?"

"In China, if we like soup, we show it like this, see?" Her grandmother noisily slurped another spoonful.

Omigod, Grace thought. She wants me to slurp my soup, too? There's no way. I can't. "Lao Lao," she said, "we don't do that in America. We have different customs."

"Of course, Grace, I know that. But you're in a Chinese home now. Don't you want to learn our Chinese customs?" Her grandmother looked at her with wide-eyed innocence.

"Sure, Lao Lao. I'm just not comfortable making noise while I eat."

"I understand. Why don't you start off slowly? Do a small sound. It will make me feel appreciated for all the hard work I did in preparing this meal."

So that's where Mom learned how to guilt trip, Grace thought. An expert taught her. She picked up her spoon, filled it with a small amount of broth, then achieved a gentle but polite slurp. "How's that?" she asked.

"Good!" Lao Lao said. "You will get louder as you practice," she added with confidence.

After soup, they both enjoyed dipping their dumplings in a spicy soy sauce. Lao Lao used her chopsticks, and Grace, the fork she found at the back of the utensil drawer. Her grandmother agreed it might take her some time to learn the art of eating with chopsticks.

Following dinner, Grace excused herself to take a shower and change into her summer night gown. It was early but she was exhausted from her trip. Having gained several hours with the time change, she was ready to go to sleep early. As she climbed into bed, she noticed that her grandmother had left something on the side table. Must have done it while I was showering, she thought. She picked up the lined pages, realizing it was the beginning of Dr. Hall's journal. Lao Lao was not only good at guilt-tripping; she was also persistent.

She opened up to the first page of the handwritten journal and noticed the elegant penmanship. Not your typical doctor's writing, Grace thought. She began to read:

> *Letter No. 1*
> *Li Man, Shansi, China*
> *August 1896*
>
> *My Dear Friends:*
>
> *I will begin my letters to you by . . .*

3

A Village in China

The next morning, Grace woke with a start. It took her a few moments to realize she wasn't home in New Jersey, sleeping in her own bed. Dr. Hall's journal was still sitting on top of the green floral duvet where it had dropped when she'd finally nodded off to sleep. She had to admit his writing was interesting. His journal took the form of a letter written to his friends back home, which gave his writing an informal style. She'd laughed when she read his explanation for what Li Man Chuang meant. According to Dr. Hall, Li meant "a prune" in Chinese, man meant "full," and Chuang was the word for "village." In other words, it meant "full of prunes village." The Chinese people sure had a way with words, she thought.

Grace learned that Li was also one of China's most common surnames, and it was given to the village as a mark of respect. Hall described the history of the village, which was once a site of overland trade with Mongolia and Russia.

The wealthy merchants, who lived there during an earlier time, competed to build the highest buildings, thus giving Li Man more tall buildings than any other village on the plain. When I have asked what made up a native's ideas of grandeur, the almost invariable response has been "a high house" (lou). Many spaces once occupied by these imposing structures are now a mass of rubbish—not worth the amount it would require to clean away. Some of this destruction was wrought by a change of route of the overland trade, but a substantial proportion of the destruction has been wrought by opium. Family after family have gone down before this monster—from positions of trust and honor, they have descended to beggars, petty thieves, and to the grave.

So much of the village, which was once a grand place, was now in ruins. Grace hadn't realized that opium was a major problem for the Chinese back then. She was curious to read more, to learn how the drug had come to China in the first place, and to discover how it had destroyed these Chinese families. But information about opium would have to wait. Dr. Hall was still describing the village where he worked. She learned houses were different by the time he arrived in Li Man in 1896. No one lived in a house with more than one story. Most homes now consisted of compounds with high walls and a large gate at the entrance. *"Safety lies in having high walls, heavy gates and sturdy locks,"* Hall wrote. Carts were allowed to enter the first court, after which small gates were used. The interior usually followed a single pattern:

The (one story) rooms are arranged around the inside of the wall, with no idea as to either comfort or convenience. It appears to me that the people think that the two important things to avoid are sunlight and fresh air. The rooms are usually dark and very close. *The only opening, in many instances, was a small aperture, a few inches square, near the top of a window. This is not so much to admit fresh air as to provide an exit for gas and smoke.*

Dr. Hall found the streets to be narrow, crooked, dirty, and a dumping ground for useless items. Very few of the estimated three thousand people who resided in Li Man lived in Chinese grandeur any longer. *"From hand to mouth is the rule, and plenty, the exception,"* he wrote.

The village stretches along the base of the mountain for nearly a mile, and from four compounds, where we live in the Southern sections, widens to eight or ten compounds at the North. The bare, stony mountains may be seen from our court. The most prominent buildings in any village are usually the temples. Li man has only one large temple, which does not speak well for the place. It is said the builders thought more of private enterprise than of the temples. The business of the village is confined mostly to one street; the stores open directly on to the street and differ from one another, more in their contents than in the outward appearance.

Dr. Hall finally wrote that he planned to tell his friends about the many stories and "folklore" he heard from his patients. First, he explained the dragon was *"universally respected and feared by these peculiar but interesting people."* The following story came about because of a violent thunderstorm that occurred one day. He noticed that a group of patients were frightened by how close the lightning was and how terrible the noise of the thunder. This is how one of their Chinese teachers explained the phenomenon to Dr. Hall:

The Dragon lives high on top of the blue sky. He guards the sun by day and the moon and stars by night. When an eclipse of the moon comes, it is he who prevents the destruction of the moon. Sometimes, he gets so close to the sun that the god of light is partially hid from sight. When the Dragon wishes rain to fall, he causes clouds to gather from all ends of the earth. The Dragon likes to ride on the clouds. The lightning is the flashings from his eyes, and the thunder is the noise made when he beats on his drum of death. That call of death is for someone in the village nearest to where he sits on the clouds. That is proven beyond a shadow of a doubt because someone always dies after a thunderstorm. Be careful of your lives when you hear the beating of his drum of death. When the call of the Dragon is heard, little children should place their open hands on the head above the ears, stoop to the earth, and cry aloud to the Dragon to pass them by. Men and women should fear the death-drum of the Dragon as a real existence, and as a constant menace to their lives.

When Dr. Hall explained to his patients that their idea of thunder was not like his, they asked the opinion of another teacher. Not wanting to commit himself in front of a foreigner, all the man would say was, *"The ideas of the People of China and the ideas of the people of foreign countries are not the same."* Hall wrote, *"I had no inclination to dispute his word."*

This was Grace's first inkling that the Chinese way of thinking in the 1800s differed greatly from that of America, even back then. The science behind the causes of thunder and lightning had nothing to do with dragons. Yet, these Chinese men believed in the dragon and saw it as a potential threat to their existence. What a frightening world to live in, she thought.

* * * * *

It surprised Grace that she enjoyed the Chinese breakfast Lao Lao made—deep-fried dough sticks dipped in a bowl of soy milk. Her grandmother called it "duòujiang yótiáo." It had a sweet taste that was pleasant, but Grace still preferred her usual breakfast, Honey Nut Cheerios with bananas and fresh blueberries. She still wasn't ready to slurp the rest of the soy milk from the bowl, but made a little noise, while her grandmother nodded approval.

"I read Dr. Hall's first journal entry," she mentioned to Lao Lao, as she wiped her lips with a paper napkin. "It was interesting. He described the village where he practiced medicine. The living conditions didn't sound too sanitary. He also explained that the village had gone downhill because people began to use opium. I think I knew that was a problem in China back then, but I didn't realize how bad it was."

"From what my parents told me, it was very bad," said

her grandmother, "but I don't know much about it. My friend, Mr. Albert Liu, will know a great deal. For many years, he taught Chinese history at the University of California, here at Berkeley. Whenever I have a question about history, he always has an answer." Lao Lao got up to clear the table. "He will be visiting us this week. Write down your questions and he will answer them for you."

"Here, let me help you," Grace said, as she rose from the kitchen table, picking up her bowl and the rest of their dishes. As she walked toward the large, white, cast-iron sink, she added, "Dr. Hall ended his letter with a story about how the Chinese at the time thought the thunder from a storm was really a dragon banging on his . . . what did he call it . . . his death drum. The people believed that someone in the village would always die after the storm. Isn't that crazy?"

"A'i, maybe not so crazy! Dragons are an important part of Chinese culture for thousands of years. In Chinese mythology, there are nine dragons, and they each have their strengths. Some are good, some not so good."

"But Lao Lao, dragons aren't real. You know that." Grace poured water into the sink with some soap.

"Of course, I know that Grace," Lao Lao said, handing her granddaughter a yellow dishrag. "I live in the modern world, but dragons are a part of my heritage. Do you want me to do away with it?" She used a matching towel to wipe the dishes Grace had rinsed and placed in the dish rack.

I guess there's no dishwasher, Grace thought.

Lao Lao continued, "There's still much we don't understand about life. Why do you think we perform the dragon dance at Chinese New Year? We believe that it scares away evil spirits. What's the harm in that?"

"It's . . . it's all superstition," Grace stammered. "I don't believe in it."

"You need to learn more," Lao Lao said, "before you can decide what to believe and what not to believe. Reading these journals will help you to understand."

"I will. I promise," Grace sighed. "But why don't we take care of your furniture problems first?"

"I have it under control, Grace. Now go back and read another journal entry," Lao Lao shooed her away from the sink with her hands. "I made an appointment to get a tour of my future living space tomorrow afternoon. Mr. Albert Liu has offered to drive us there. We will invite him to dine with us afterwards. Save your questions about China's history for then."

Grace returned to her bedroom, frustrated. She grabbed Dr. Hall's journal and sat in the Monk chair next to the side table. Before she began, her grandmother swept into the room with an armful of papers.

"I brought you more of Dr. Hall's writings," she said. "In case you finish what you have. I must make a few phone calls and create a list of my furniture. I'll see you at lunch." With that, she hurried out.

Grace frowned, sat back in the Monk chair, and began her reading, as commanded. Dr. Hall continued his journal with some facts about Chinese New Year, which were very confusing to him and had nothing to do with a new year as he understood it. To begin with, it always seemed to occur at the start of a current emperor's reign, whenever that was. The Chinese even recorded important events from the past, saying the event happened during the reign of whatever emperor ruled at the time. To make matters more confusing, calendar years were not always the same length. He pointed out that the previous year had contained thirteen months, because there were two separate fifth months. Dr. Hall admitted he never could keep track. Grace couldn't blame him.

The "New Year" is the birthday of the Empire. It appears that everything is expected to begin anew with the beginning of a new year. I am told that it is the custom to settle all business affairs once a year, just before the new year dawns. Any affairs not so adjusted must go over for another year or be forgotten forever. The last few days of the year are busy days. On the streets, in the shops, along the highways they go, the pursuing and the pursued. This condition of affairs is all the more interesting, when it is known that all that is necessary for a man to do, when he does not wish to settle a bill, is to just keep out of reach of the man to whom he owes the debt. Extra efforts are made to collect debts. Some of the plans used are inhuman, consisting of torture, insults, and supplications, strangely commingled. And the efforts to escape payment are just as strange and unreasonable.

Dr. Hall heard a few stories about people who tried to avoid payment of their debts. One story involved an old man who had an amusing plan to avoid paying his bill. He took advantage of a custom to prepare extra food for the feast of the kitchen god.

He and his wife occupied a room in a court with other families. Food was brought, as usual, for the offering (to the kitchen god), but instead of giving it to the god, the old people stored their share away in their room. The door was then fastened on the inside, and the occupants of the room awaited developments. Soon, a man came into the court with a bill. Our hero positively refused to see the man! Then others came. Each tried his persuasive powers, but to no avail. Threats, bribes, pleadings, excitement in the court and in the street proved alike useless. On the third day, just before dark, a man carrying a package came into the court. He announced in loud tones that it was for our heroine, from her dearly beloved son, who was away in another province. Two pairs of eyes peeped thru the window. Yes, there sat the box. What could be in it? The latch is stealthily withdrawn and the mother hobbles out to receive her gift. How her heart must have throbbed when she beheld such a large box and all her own! But she was destined never to reach the box. The men were too quick for her, and she was their prisoner.

Grace chuckled. She loved that Dr. Hall had described the

old man and his wife as "our hero" and "our heroine," and couldn't wait to read what happened next.

Now our hero would surely come out rather than see the sharer of his joys and sorrows suffer. No, nothing was further from his thoughts. He rather enjoyed or seemed to, his lonely vigil. Outside the door was an old tree. This tree stood nearer the prison-home than any other room. During the afternoon of the last day, there was a great commotion in the court. A man was seen tying a rope around his neck, and then he threw the other end over a limb. He said someone in the court had injured him, and he was going to die as nigh as possible to the origin of his disgrace. Again, the eyes appeared, but now only one pair was seen. The man stepped onto a chair and gently swung off. This was a serious matter. The man would be found dead nearer our hero's room than any other, and he would be responsible. This was too much for the old man. He opened the door, rushed out to cut the rope, and ran into the arms of his creditors. All at once, the would-be-suicide changed his mind, and our friend was borne in triumph from the court.

Grace laughed out loud. Dr. Hall was a delightful storyteller. He made her feel as if she were there in the court, watching it all happen. The next story he told, about a man who tried to avoid paying his debt, actually occurred to the good doctor.

A *few days before the end of the last year, a man came to the dispensary, seeking treatment for a sore toe. The toe was seen, and I told the man he could care for it at his home if he wished. He said he did not want to go home. He had heard of the wonderful skill of the foreign physician and wanted to stay near. He was assigned a room, and I did what I could for him. The toe had to be removed. The man suffered untold agony, he said, before he came. After the new year, he wanted to go home. The toe was in bad condition, and I did not want him to go. He returned to his home and, on inquiry, some of the other patients told me the man had himself run an iron needle through his toe, three times. His intention was to have an excuse for remaining indoors, when the time for paying debts should come. He was afraid he was going to die and came to me for relief. By leaving home, he missed the visits of his creditors, and as the chief cause for his distress was removed by the coming of the new year, he felt he could go home in peace.*

Dr. Hall had been taken in by the man, but he seemed to forgive him, Grace thought. He believed that the old man in the first story and his patient in the second didn't see themselves as dishonest. *"Their standards of integrity were not so high as ours,"* he wrote. He made a point of writing that most Chinese people were honorable and tried to repay their loans. As a medical missionary, he hoped that the teachings of Christianity someday would be their guide, helping them to understand more and give up their questionable customs. What a generous, patient, caring man, Grace realized.

Wanting to learn more about this extraordinary Dr. Hall, Grace continued on to his next journal entry. The doctor couldn't get over the simplicity of the people he encountered in China. He didn't feel that their problems arose from malice, but more from ignorance. Although he did his best to help them, they stubbornly held on to their superstitious beliefs and were reluctant to search for the truth. If they would only take the time to investigate, Hall felt, they would see their beliefs were not rational. As an example, he told the story of the fox spirit, a popular creature in Chinese mythology for over two thousand years.

According to legend, the fox had the power of transformation on a certain night during a specific time in the cycle of the moon. Any man who witnessed this change would be overpowered by the vision. Dr. Hall wrote:

On certain nights during this moon, this animal is said to appear as a most beautiful woman. The change is wrought in an instant. Fire in two long flames issues from its mouth, the eyes flash and grow bright, until the sight of the spectator is overpowered by the radiance thereof. Then the change comes. Only for a few minutes, just after midnight, may this be witnessed. And fortunate is the man who sees the change. I asked several men if this was a fact, and they all answered in the affirmative. 'Have you ever witnessed the change?' 'No! I have not, but I have heard of men who had been fortunate.' Thus, it goes. The people do not try to investigate such a thing. Superstition, associated as it is with ignorance and an utter lack of the spirit of investigation, proves a barrier to understanding.

How frustrating it must have been for Dr. Hall, Grace thought, to explain the science behind his healing while the Chinese people clung to their superstitions. But it seemed there was more to the story.

During this moon, the fox has the power of healing all diseases. The great obstacle, in the way of all the people taking advantage of his wondrous skill, was the difficulty experienced in meeting him. But the people believe he can heal diseases, for men have said, until they were treated by the fox, their complaints were many—now the body has no illness at all. When a man is bewitched, he (also) acquires a peculiar power. He can treat Diphtheria! Lucky the village which has a fox-man, should it be visited by this dread disease. He alone can fight the evil demon-dragon which brings Diphtheria.

There's that dragon again, thought Grace. One of the nine that Lao Lao talked about. This must be a bad one. Dr. Hall went on to describe how the village of Li Man was cursed by the dragon, and the Diphtheria came.

Liman had no fox-man to treat or prevent the ravages of the scourge. Men and women, as well as the children, fell before it. As a last resort, an application was made to the magistrate for relief. He issued this order:"Any compound which has had ten cases of Diphtheria may claim to have a fox-man!" Less than three hundred yards from our gate, by the great gate of an extensive compound, I saw a small block of wood nailed to the wall. On this is written two (Chinese) characters, giving notice to the demon-dragon that the compound had a fox-man. The dragon, on seeing these characters, dares not enter.

Dr. Hall discovered that the man who lived there had bought it from the magistrate as a warning. A few days later, when Hall was trying to explain to a patient *"the functions of the brain and its relations to the different portions of the body,"* he got an even clearer idea of how the Chinese people thought:

On saying to him that reason and government and emotion and passion were supposed to originate in the brain, (the patient) replied, "No, doctor, you are all wrong. The seat of reason and love and passion is not in the head, but in the stomach! There are only two exceptions to this rule. The cock reasons from its comb. The first faint rays of light strike its comb, and it immediately announces the approach of day. The wolf's reason is neither in its head nor in its body, but in its legs. When the wolf sees the image of a dragon, its legs immediately drag his body around and make *off with it." The lesson was postponed to some future indefinite time!*

At least Dr. Hall had a good sense of humor, Grace thought as she smiled. And yet, there was a perverse sense to the logic of his Chinese patient, who thought the cock reasons from its comb, since the early light of day hits its comb first. But she could tell from Hall's writing that these obstacles to his missionary and medical work saddened him. He believed it was necessary to overthrow the superstitions of these simple-minded people in order to help them. Also, he found the people were an odd mixture of superstition and contradiction. They had many gods, whom you'd expect to be wise and flawless in their view, but some of the wisest ones proved to be gullible.

To illustrate, the kitchen god is very fond of a certain kind of candy. The people, knowing his weakness for this particular sweet-meat, take advantage of his godship in a most unkind way. It would never do for this god to go up to heaven and tell of all their sins of omission and commission. The god's throat is small. The people prepare this candy in round hollow balls, small enough to go into his mouth, but too large to enter the throat. These balls are placed with the other offerings. The god, on seeing his favorite, immediately fills his mouth. It will not go down and he will not give it up, so away to heaven he must go, with his mouth so full it is not possible to say a word. Poor old god! And yet, these people think of this same kitchen

god as their patron saint! They fall down before his
image and make obeisance as tho' their lives and their
happiness depended on his gracious pleasure.

Another great story, Grace thought, as she wondered how well Dr. Hall had succeeded in bringing Christian beliefs to China. She set aside the journal, turned on her laptop, and looked up religion in China today. She knew from a class in college that Taoism, Confucianism, and Buddhism had been the early religions of China, and had continued, but she hadn't realized that Chinese folk religion had intertwined with all three. When Christianity came along, it was tough going. China was a large and complicated country. The number of people who practiced any of these religions varied from province to province, so it was difficult to tell how many Christians there were.

Of course, atheism was the official belief system of China now. She wondered if people were even allowed to practice religion. She discovered there was a period when they weren't, but the government now recognized the existence of religious practices. In fact, some scholars today acknowledged the value of folk religion because it helped to preserve traditional culture. In fact, folk religion was still the most practiced religion in China. Her grandmother said these stories were part of her heritage. Maybe she was right.

It seemed that Christianity was still practiced by a small percentage of people in China but had been growing lately. Maybe Dr. Hall's wish would come true after one hundred twenty years. A part of her hoped so.

Grace was curious to learn where Shansi province was in

China but couldn't find it. She eventually figured out what is called Shanxi Province today was probably the same. She learned that the Chinese language does not use the Romanized system of letters that other languages use. Over the past few decades, the spelling of many names was changed to make it easier for those cultures to pronounce them correctly. For instance, what was once Peking is now Beijing. She couldn't find the village of Li Man. It was probably too small to find on the maps she had access to online.

From force of habit, she grabbed her notebook to record what she'd learned so far. Reading Dr. Hall's journals had given her something to think about. He was an extraordinary man, who had given up a comfortable life in his own country to help people who lived in a world so different from his. And he wasn't even Chinese himself. She realized she wanted to learn more about his experiences. Did he write about the practice of Chinese medicine at the time? What was the relationship between men and women? What was it like to be a kid growing up in China? How did he deal with the problem of opium? And why was there such a problem with opium in the first place? Grace wanted to know more.

4

"FEAR COLD" AND BONES

H t lunch that day, Lao Lao decided it was time for Grace to learn to use chopsticks. "It's easy," she said, showing her how to hold the lower chopstick in the crook between her thumb and first finger and touching her ring finger. "The lower chopstick never moves," she explained. Satisfied that Grace was holding it correctly, she demonstrated how to hold the upper chopstick between her first and second finger, pressing it firmly with her thumb on her first finger and making sure that the ends matched. "You see, the thumb holds the upper chopstick in place. Only the upper chopstick moves to meet the lower one. Be careful not to bend your thumb or the lower chopstick will fall," her grandmother warned.

Grace practiced moving the upper chopstick toward the lower, several times. "It doesn't seem too difficult, Lao Lao," she said.

"Good," her grandmother replied. "Now you can practice with your lunch." She showed her how, by picking up a pork and cabbage dumpling, dipping it into a sauce, and placing it in her mouth. "Mmm . . . it's delicious."

Grace followed her example, being careful not to bend her thumb, and, after some fumbling, placed the dumpling in her mouth—on the third try. "Yes, I did it!" The following two bites were easier.

"Next, I will teach you how to eat rice," Lao Lao said, picking up the bowl of rice she had placed on the table. "Chinese people pick up their rice bowls with their hands and hold them close to their mouths, so nothing falls. First, you must dig into the rice, then you pull up a small amount and put it in your mouth. Some people make it easier by shoveling the rice into their mouths. I don't think it's very polite, do you?"

"No, Lao Lao," Grace answered. But slurping your food is ok, she thought with amusement. After a few attempts, Grace got some rice into her mouth. By the end of lunch, she was tempted to shovel it in, but controlled herself. Thank goodness the dumplings were easy and filling.

As Grace took her dishes to the sink, her grandmother asked, "How is the reading going? Are you enjoying Dr. Hall's journals?"

"I wouldn't say I'm 'enjoying' them," she replied, looking at her grandmother. "But they're interesting, I'll give you that. Even Dr. Hall doesn't approve of all their superstitions. You won't believe some of the stories he tells. He treated a man who'd pushed three needles through one of his toes, just to avoid repaying a debt. I mean, that's crazy. The poor guy ended up losing his toe. But he was happy because he'd avoided paying what he owed."

Lao Lao grunted. "There are a few people like that in every culture, don't you think? People who are dishonorable and will go to great lengths to avoid what's expected of them."

"I don't know. Pushing a needle through your toe is kind of extreme." Grace frowned. "I'd like to know more about the way Dr. Hall handled his patients."

"In that case," her grandmother said, "you'd better get back to your reading. I'll clean up in here."

Returning to her room again, Grace picked up where she'd left off. After reading a few pages, she was happy to see that Dr. Hall had written about his medical practice in China.

During the year, I saw and treated one thousand eight hundred and sixty-eight cases. These patients come from far and near—if one patient comes from a village, we expect more. Diseases, which to these people seem beyond remedy, are often entirely cured, and all evidence thereof removed with cleanliness and the application of simple remedies. One of our first duties appears to be to impress on the minds of the patients that cleanliness is essential to recovery.

That's surprising, thought Grace. Keeping a wound clean had always been a rule of thumb, growing up. Any time she fell and skinned her knee, her mother would wash off the dirt and apply an antiseptic, before adding a Band-Aid. It was difficult to fathom that the Chinese at the time didn't grasp that. She soon learned that they didn't just misunderstand the need for a clean wound. They were actually afraid of cleanliness. Dr. Hall explained:

A patient comes to me with a wound on the hand, caused by running a chisel into the flesh. To look at the man, with his whole arm wrapped and bundled, it would seem that he feared a death-wound. I first remove the garment wrapped around the outside. Then I find the long sleeves (all of them) brought down over the hand and a string tied around the ends. After many protests from the patient—"fear cold, fear cold", and many assurances by me, "no fear, no fear", he unties the string. He slowly loosens out the folds, glances around the room to see if it has any openings for cold to enter, and asks if the door is securely fastened. He asks if I expect to run a needle thro' his hand (the Chinese way of treating all diseases—run a long iron or silver needle into the seat of disease, to kill the evil spirit who has taken up its abode in that part), or give medicine to rub on or to take internally, etc.

Dr. Hall insisted he needed to see the actual wound and threatened to make him leave to make room for other patients if he resisted. Against his better judgment, the patient pulled his sleeves up to his elbow, revealing a cloth bag just large enough to fit around the hand. Dr. Hall continued:

After we convince the man that all must be removed, he takes his hand out of the bag, removes the cloths that are wound and wound around it, and at last holds up his hand for inspection. As yet, I can see nothing except a mass of black. The hand was covered with black dirt, or coal dust, when he received the wound, and had not been disturbed. I cannot describe to you, on paper, the expressions of that face, and the ohs and ahs when the assistant turns a stream of warm water on to the hand. Do we dare use water? After the hand is clean—I find the wound. It was small at first, but pus formed and, unable to escape, had burrowed in among the tendons and around the bones."How many days?"I ask.

"Eighteen."

"No wonder it is in bad condition! We use a simple dressing, bind it up lightly, and the man goes away happy. A few dressings usually restore the hand to its natural condition. I give this instance, not as an exception, but as a type of what we see. Let the wound be what it will, let the disease be in any part of the body. It is a task for the patient to risk his life by exposing himself to "cold." The day may be sultry, but that mysterious something, designated "cold," is ever present.

Grace put down the journal. She was stunned by the patient's lack of understanding when it came to cleanliness and fresh air. But he could only be healed by giving up his fears and following Hall's advice. Why were these people afraid of cleanliness? No wonder Dr. Hall found them so frustrating. Unreasonable superstitions weren't just a bar to teaching Christianity; they were also a hindrance to their health.

At that moment, Lao Lao passed the door to her room. "Lao Lao," she called. "Wait until you hear this." She then told her the story she'd just read. "Isn't that crazy?"

Lao Lao smiled. "Only as crazy as the people who are afraid of having surgery. Or those who fear going to the dentist to get rid of a toothache. There are people who are afraid of heights or tight places or flying or going out in public. Have you ever avoided "walking under a ladder," or "knocked on wood" when you hoped for something? There are people like that all over the world, Grace. The Chinese are not the only ones susceptible to fear and superstition."

"But . . ." Grace tried to think of a good argument, then gave up. Lao Lao had won this round. She was more astute than Grace had realized. After her grandmother left, still smiling, Grace returned to her reading, wondering what other oddities the good doctor had encountered about the rural Chinese in his practice. It wasn't long before she discovered it—bones!

Dr. Hall soon noticed that the Chinese were hesitant about having a bone, or part of a bone, removed. They had a fixed idea of being buried together with all their bones. Hall told one story about a patient whose leg had been crushed by a heavy stone.

He spent ten days consulting with relatives, friends, and native healers. They brought him to us as a last resort. His body was hot all the time. When he tried to say words, they came reluctantly and were not easily understood. He had taken no food for five days. Even a bowl of hot water refused to stay down his throat. His condition was indescribably filthy. The only wonder was that he was living. The weather was hot. The flies were beyond number. The leg was amputated. Strict agreement was made that the leg should not be destroyed. It must, at all hazards, be kept to go to the grave with the balance of his body whenever the gods should demand his soul for another.

The clinic found someone to take the amputated leg to the patient's home while he recuperated at the clinic. After a while, a strange odor coming from the man's room kept all the nurses busy changing dressings and sterilizing. The stump appeared perfectly healthy, and we could find no reason for such an unpleasant ending to what had seemed a reasonably perfect result. Soon, other patients were complaining. Matters became so unsatisfactory we had the man carried out into the court and all bedding removed from the room. (The truth was soon revealed.) After the man was engaged to go away with the leg, the patient decided that it must not be separated from the balance of his bones. He had wrapped the leg in an old garment and was using it for a pillow! His excuse was that, should the leg be destroyed or lost, he would have to travel all thru the future state of existence, a crippled, dishonored spirit.

To the Chinese, bones included their teeth. This was a distinct problem when patients came with aching teeth, and the only answer to their pain was to remove them. The results were often amusing.

A woman, whose tooth dropped out when I took hold of it with my fingers, flew into a great passion, cried, and spat at her serving woman by turns, and pounded the floor with her stick. (I think she wanted to pound the doctor.) On inquiry, I learned that she came to have the tooth fastened, not removed.

An old man, whose two remaining teeth I would not guarantee to "eat food," went away, turning them lovingly this way and that with his tongue, assuring me that "I want not to separate my bones." He had all his other teeth carefully wrapped and carried them with him wherever he went, and his family had strict orders to place them all in his coffin to go to the grave with the balance of his body, after the gods had taken back his soul.

What a strange custom, Grace reflected. Then again, she recalled that reincarnation was a Buddhist belief. Maybe these people believed it was necessary to keep all their bones for their next life. She had a feeling Dr. Hall's sense of humor would pull him through these episodes, and she was right.

Many such interesting cases are met, some arousing mirth, but the great majority awaking pity. The people are grateful for services rendered. I know, and some of their simple demonstrations go right to our hearts.

It was then that Hall and his staff would speak to their

patients about the joys of heaven. He hoped that accepting Christian beliefs would rid them of superstitions.

It is not for us to know the result of the year's work. We know that the future holds much in store for this Empire. The time is coming when China will be called Christian—our faith is strong in the promises.

Grace supposed the doctor would be disappointed to learn that only a small percentage of Chinese people were Christian today. But she was sure he'd be delighted to find out that the number was increasing. He had such optimism about drawing the Chinese people out of the dark ages and into a better future. She wondered what the state of medicine was like in China today. Did Dr. Hall and the other medical missionaries make a difference?

Just then, the phone rang. It was her mother.

"Hi Mom," Grace said.

"Hello, Grace. I was wondering how you and your grandmother are doing."

"Okay, I guess. She taught me how to eat with chopsticks today."

Her mother laughed. "How did that go?"

"It wasn't as hard as I thought it would be." Grace hesitated a moment. "Mom, can I ask you something?"

"Sure, Grace. What is it?"

"Don't get mad, Mom, but I was wondering why you stopped visiting Lao Lao. And why you never talk about your past . . . about growing up."

Grace heard a deep sigh from her mother. "That's a fair question, Grace. I guess there are a few things you should know. Your grandfather owned a gift store in San Francisco's Chinatown. The store, where your grandmother also worked, sold Asian antiques and Chinese clothing," said Julia.

"I know. Lao Lao told me."

"We lived in an apartment above it and your grandfather rented out the other two floors to Chinese families."

"You lived in Chinatown when you were a kid?" Grace was surprised. She hadn't made the connection.

"Yes, and I hated it. I was expected to help at the store after school. I had to dust their precious antiques, sweep the floor, and refold the Chinese clothing that had been picked over—before I was allowed to start my homework. I was also forced to go to Chinese school every Saturday, so I could learn Mandarin. I did it for eight years."

"You can speak Mandarin?"

"Much good it did me." Her mother sighed again. "You know those red envelopes you got from your grandmother on Chinese New Year? It was more than that. It was our time to honor the gods and our ancestors who'd gone before us. First, we had to clean the house to get rid of bad luck and get ready for the good luck of the new year. We had a whole list of chores, from hanging red lanterns to putting up paper cuttings and short Chinese poetry. Offering sacrifices to ancestors, giving red envelopes with money, fireworks, dragon dances, lucky food to eat, a special reunion dinner—they were all part of it. Everything was red because red is China's lucky color. I admit I enjoyed it for a time. Then my life changed on the first day of the Chinese New Year, the year I turned twelve. Your grandfather had a heart attack and died. After all we'd done to get rid of bad luck. Ha! That's when I realized it was all superstition. There's no way you can guarantee good luck in your life."

Grace couldn't speak.

Her mom continued, "My mother sold the store and the building. With a portion of the money, she bought an old house in Berkeley. I missed my father terribly, and she was never the same. Living alone with her wasn't easy. Whatever warmth she had for me left when my father died. I had to go back to the city for the next two years to finish my Mandarin studies. When it came time for college, I chose a school as far away from her as I could get. That's how I ended up living in New Jersey. You see, Grace, I didn't want you to fall for all the superstitions I'd grown up with, so I never talked about my past."

"I get the picture. These journals I've been reading talk a lot about Chinese superstitions, especially those of the people living in a particular village in Shansi Province in 1896. Trust me, your superstitions don't even begin to compare. These people even thought keeping their wounds clean was dangerous. You're right. Believing in superstitions isn't good. Even the doctor who wrote the journals agreed."

"Then you understand," her mother said.

"I do. But then Lao Lao pointed out that people all over the world have superstitions they believe. It's not just a Chinese problem."

"I guess it's true."

"Maybe if we see those superstitions, not as a reality, but as an illustration of our cultural identity, we can accept them more easily. For example, how many Irish people actually believe in leprechauns? But they love to tell stories about them. Does that make sense?"

"Yes, Grace, it does. You're saying I should rethink my culture and learn to embrace it, but in a different way."

"Otherwise, aren't you negating thousands of years of your cultural history, Mom?"

"When did you get to be so smart, Grace?"

"It didn't come from me, Mom. It came from Lao Lao. She told me not to jump to any conclusions about superstitions."

"I see," her mother answered.

"Gotta go, Mom." Grace picked up the journal. "I think Dr. Hall is about to tell me about Chinese medicine during his stay in China."

"You mean acupuncture?" her mother asked.

"After what I've read so far, I doubt it'll be as simple as that. Bye, Mom."

Grace was right. She hadn't forgotten the patient who wanted to know if Dr. Hall was going to insert a needle into his wound to release the bad spirits, a common medical practice. He had seen two Chinese doctors in action at a fair in a large market town near Li Man. The doctors had a tent where they were treating people of *"any and all diseases."* What Grace read next shocked her even more.

5

The Gentle Art of Healing

The tent where the doctors worked was on one of the main streets of the fair. From the front of the tent, many banners were hanging, proclaiming the doctors' great skills at curing different diseases.

On one large banner is the information that all diseases of bones were as quickly cured as it was easy to blow out a rush-light. The stomach reaches up with joy to partake of the delightful mixtures made ready for the ailments, striking that most important organ of the human body. Pains of the head are as dreams that are done, when once they meet the powerful remedies made to attack them where they live. Eyes all dark to light shine as the moon when the things we do are made known to them. Legs that have forgotten the way to carry the body, leap and run when their owners are brought into close relationship with our great skill. Our skillful hands make old men young and young men wise.

It was clear, Grace thought, that modesty was not a feature of the two men. One doctor was a specialist on diseases above the waist, the other on ailments below. Hall watched as the first doctor operated on a patient who, according to Dr. Hall, had a *"simple inflammation of the eye."* Grace read the description with horror.

He asked the name of the patient, the year of his birth, felt both pulses, asked the name of the animal under which he was born, then glanced at the eye. He muttered some ancient formula, made a few passes with a wand before the man's face, and announced that the patient was all ready to be healed.

He then pinched up the skin on the forehead, over the nose, took up a silver needle about six inches long, thrust it through the skin and brought it out on the other side, possibly an inch from the place of insertion. Next, taking up the cheek, he thrust a needle thru it. The point entered about a half inch from the angle of the mouth, passing thru the cheek into the mouth, point carried backward toward the angle of the jaw, and brought it out thru the flesh as near the ear as possible. The point of the needle was then elevated and passed over the ear on the outside. The other cheek was treated in the same fashion.

The Chinese doctor wasn't finished yet!

He then used a small rod of iron as follows: placing one end of the iron rod firmly against the temple, he held the other end in his hand, with the back of his hand pressed firmly against his shoulder. With his right hand, he then drew what seemed to be another iron rod, with links attached, rapidly *back and forth across the rod held against the head, and at right angles to that iron. This noisy, rasping maneuver kept up for at least thirty seconds. Then the operator, dropping the iron, rod, chain, and all, sprang to a small table standing near, grasped something between his thumb and forefinger, jumped back to his patient and thrust a small metal dart, with a head like an upholstery tack, but larger, into the spot where the iron had rested. The impinge against the skull gave forth an unpleasant sound. The other temple received the same routine treatment.*

Grace shuddered at this vivid picture. Dr. Hall, once again, made her feel as if she were there, watching the man's treatment.

There were, now, (1) one needle thru the forehead, (2) one needle thru each cheek, and (3) one thru each temple. Now, an incense stick, about three inches long, lighted at one end, was laid over (resting on top of) each ear. This burned slowly away, the patient sitting immovable—unmoved by any part of the operation. When the points of the needles were white hot, they were withdrawn with a jerk, then those in the temples were removed, and, last of all, that from the forehead. The patient was pronounced "cured." The healer collected his fee, turned to another patient, made a few passes before his face, asked him a few questions, and said, "this man is ready to be healed."

Grace found this barbaric method of treatment alarming. Did these people really believe that evil spirits had caused their illnesses? And why did this bizarre attempt to remove the evil spirits need to be so cruel? She soon learned that the people were not just fascinated by the doctor's treatments, but couldn't wait to have it done to themselves.

The scene may be described in a few sentences, but no power on earth can describe the tight-lipped, adoring, admiring, believing, wondering crowd pressed close to witness the miraculous skill of the great healers. The men seeking relief stood in line, two deep, for hours, waiting their turn to be healed. The uproar of the fair was usually as sweet music to their ears and sights of beauty to their eyes, but this show was best of all. With their own eyes, they made witness to the wonders of the day. Off to one side, huddled close together, waited many tens of women and children. There they waited, and so far as I could learn, not one was called to the presence of the great men. They were not interested in women and children.

The good doctor added one final insight.

The copper coins given as fees were all thrown on a camel's hair mat, spread out in front of the tent. The fees were paid to the door attendant. No coin ever touched the hand of the healer. An immense pile of cash proved to all lookers-on that the men doing the healing were at least good collectors.

Grace had to stop and catch her breath. She couldn't believe the way these barbaric, so-called doctors took advantage of the Chinese people. The women and children were lucky to be ignored by them. Dr. Hall must have been beside himself when he witnessed this scene. How were the Chinese doctors able to get away with it? She was sure that many of the people they treated must have died. The next story Grace read gave her an answer.

"Fool, of course the man will die! You have turned the needle the wrong way." This was one Chinese physician's way of shifting responsibility for a patient's death to an assistant.

Although the man had experienced illness in the past, he'd appeared healthy only one week before. He'd gone to the fair, but soon felt a strange sensation take over his body. He couldn't raise his left hand or move his right leg. He also couldn't speak words that made sense, and his head swayed from side to side. His friends took him to a doctor at the fair who determined his situation was *"dangerous."* The *"medicine-soup"* the doctor prescribed did not heal him, so his friends called on a famous *"cure-all"* who was visiting the fair.

This great healer came in all the dignity due to his high calling. The great healer said all the other doctors were wrong. He alone could make a proper diagnosis—he alone could name the disease correctly. Then he readily, without the loss of a second of time, located the seat of the trouble and gave it a name. Having made a correct diagnosis and located the cause, the treatment became a thing of minor importance.

A small sore gave the doctor his cue. He ran a long needle into the knee joint, and with the help of a few bystanders, some pulling at the head and some at the feet, he succeeded in making the point of the needle show on the other side of the knee. After collecting his fee, he called a young man from the crowd and placed the man in his care. I then gave orders to turn the needle at regular intervals—and always to the right.

When the doctor returned and saw that the patient was getting worse, he accused his assistant of turning the needle the wrong way. The young man insisted he'd followed his instructions carefully and always turned the needle to the right. The "cure-all" doctor then asked, "Which hand did you use to turn it?"

"I used my left hand once."

"Pity, pity, the man will die! You should have used your right hand all the time. It is readily to be seen that you know nothing of the gentle art of healing. I must go. I return to my own home tonight."

The man died—despite of all the treatments thrust into him. A cerebral hemorrhage was the plain cause of his passing from life.

Grace exploded with a "Ha!" The gentle art of healing? There's always a way to get out of trouble when the people around you aren't clever. She felt sorry for the young man who probably believed he was responsible for the man's death. Dr. Hall revealed even more about native Chinese medicine.

Being treated at fairs was the only time that people paid a fee to a doctor. Most of the time, the healer didn't charge for his services. If a family needed a healer, they sent *"a chair, or a cart, or a donkey,"* whatever they could afford, for the healer to ride on, and an attendant to accompany him. And there were rules to follow.

To lend importance to the transit to the home of the patient, this attendant must walk in front of the doctor, carrying his huge umbrella, on which are written a number of his virtues and a list of his wonderful cures. On arrival, he must be shown the greatest deference, must have a private room for his meditations—and opium—and a servant must be in constant attendance. Food must be sent in at regular intervals. Provision must be made for his entertainment if he remains on the case until the patient has fully recovered. Common report has it that very few doctors decide to remain in a home, unless there is abundant evidence of wealth and signs of liberality.

Besides using needles to treat people, the healer would write prescriptions, which must be paid for in advance. Hall found these *"credit remedies both uncertain and dangerous."* Why? Because these liquids weren't sold in medicine shops. They had to be prepared in the presence of the person who was taking them.

Every prescription must contain licorice root. Polypharmacy, the use of many remedies in one prescription, aims to strike at the root of any disease, sooner or later. The doctor uses barks of trees and buds and berries. To these he adds such savory morsels as eyes of scorpions and hearts of fowl, while bits of shell and hair and skin, added for their special action, help the bones of tigers and skeletons of crickets to give health and strength to stricken bodies. (Grace thought it sounded like a Shakespearean witch's brew.) All prescribed remedies must be mixed in designated ways to avoid changing their intended action. The mass is placed in a vessel of iron or clay, water is added, the whole is boiled for a named period of time, and the patient ordered to take a certain number of bowls of the mixture each day. One man, ordered to take twenty-one bowls of the vile mixture, said his stomach tried to crawl out thru his mouth after the nineteenth bowl—and he was afraid to take the other two doses.

Of course, after being healed, the patient was expected to send a gift to the doctor. If this didn't happen in due time, agents from the doctor would remind him he should feel grateful that the evil spirits had been *"driven away"* and show his gratitude. This harassment could go on for a while until a sufficiently valuable gift was sent. The only recourse an unsatisfied family had was to claim damages against a doctor if he allowed three family members to die. Grace didn't know whether to laugh or to cry.

Native barbers played a unique role in the preparation of the prescription medicines. They carried baskets with them, as they walked the streets, looking for customers. Once they set up shop somewhere, they saved the hair taken from their customers' heads and placed it in the baskets. Eventually, they sold the hair to medicine-makers.

To Dr. Hall's dismay, the hair was used to create a *"vile-smelling"* black paste.

> . . . *a well-nigh universal remedy for skin eruptions, aches, pains and ulcerous sores. People came to the hospital all plastered over—heads, backs, chests, stomachs, limbs—with this concoction. We discovered a liberal use of turpentine was the only way to clean it off.*

> *The recipe involved heating the hair with water and pine or fir leaves until it reached the right consistency. Then it was pulled by hand, like taffy, and applied to a piece of dog-skin. Once applied, the manufacturer has his product ready for the ultimate consumer. One barber, the first time he shaved me, debated for a long time whether he should put my hair in the common receptacle. When closely questioned, he admitted he did not know the effect the hair of a foreigner, and a white man, might have on the potency of the remedy.*

Finally, Hall wrote about the one female healer he met and

her unique remedies. Pains of the stomach interested her the most since she'd suffered from them all her life. The first of her remedies, she insisted, was always successful:

> Whenever the pain in her stomach reached the point where endurance was out of the question, she called for a bowl of hot water. Removing the wrappings from her bound feet, she washed them in the hot water. Her dutiful son, ever ready to do her bidding, then drank the water—and, in time, the stomach pain was much less! This same dutiful son had once carved a slice out of his own side and eaten the flesh, when a bit of human flesh had been ordered by a healer, as a remedy for a dreadful pain in her knee. Within a half-moon, she saw the pain was much better—thus proving to her satisfaction the great efficacy of the remedy. Broth prepared from the parings of her fingernails was another favorite remedy. It was a specific for itching skin diseases. The son drank the broth, and the mother's skin ceased its itching—after a time—and the son was all the time laying up virtue for himself by serving that one who had given him birth.

By now, Grace had lost her appetite. She apologized to Lao Lao and said she wasn't feeling well. When her grandmother suggested some noodle soup for healing, Grace held up her hand. Her head was swimming with images of needles pushed through cheeks, eyes of scorpions, hair turned into a sticky paste, and broth made from someone's fingernails. "Thanks, but I'm not feeling well, Lao Lao. I'm afraid anything I eat right now will come right back up. I think I'll go to bed early."

"Whatever you say, Grace. Too bad I made such a delicious dinner."

There was no way Grace could be guilted into eating tonight. "Sorry, but no. Goodnight, Lao Lao," she said as she headed toward her bedroom.

Before she went to sleep, Grace opened her laptop again and looked up traditional Chinese medicine called TCM, checking to see what the National Institute of Health (NIH) had to say about it. She learned it had been around for thousands of years and had been used to treat various diseases and symptoms in China. It's based on the belief, derived from Taoism, that qi (the body's vital energy) flows along meridians or channels in the body and keeps a person's spiritual, emotional, mental, and physical health in balance. It has also become more modernized since the late 1800s and includes acupuncture and tai chi, as well as the use of herbal products. Many people use it today, including Americans.

According to the NIH, Grace discovered, acupuncture is a technique in which practitioners stimulate specific parts of the body, usually by inserting thin needles through the skin. Some studies show it may ease certain types of pain, especially ones that are chronic. Grace stopped to think for a moment. Maybe the rural doctors she'd read about, the ones who used needles in barbaric ways, mistakenly thought they were using acupuncture.

She learned that tai chi combined certain postures, movements, mental focus, breathing, and relaxation. Research suggested it improved balance and stability in older people and in people with Parkinson's, as well as reduced some knee and back pains. Chinese herbal products, in the meantime, had been studied for many medical problems, but no firm conclusions could be made about their effectiveness. Also, some herbal products might be contaminated, making them potentially dangerous. The good news was that acupuncture and tai chi were pretty safe.

Grace then looked up medical missionaries during the 1800s and realized that Dr. Hall was not the only one appalled by the treatments of the Chinese rural doctors. Maybe his greatest contribution was that he and the other medical missionaries were the first to introduce western medicine to the Chinese. Because of them, medical schools were built in China during the early 1900s, and medical treatment improved. No longer were remedies passed down from one family member to another, or from a Chinese doctor to his apprentice.

Like Dr. Hall, the medical missionaries seemed to care about their patients and made it their business to understand the cultural history behind rural Chinese medicine and accept its significance to the people. As a result, medicine in China today combined the practices of both eastern and western medicine.

Grace fell asleep, at peace knowing that life had improved for the descendants of the people in the village of Li Man in the Shansi Province.

6

A "Monster" Drug

race was not prepared for the breakfast she received the next morning. She was expecting Chinese food, of course, with chopsticks for a utensil. Instead, a bowlful of Honey Nut Cheerios, a side dish of blueberries and sliced bananas, and a small pitcher of milk sat at her usual place. She even had a spoon to eat it with. Her grandmother had asked her yesterday morning what she usually ate at home, but Grace had forgotten. She now looked at Lao Lao in surprise.

"Don't look at me that way," her grandmother said. "I've lived in this country most of my life. I know what Americans eat for breakfast."

"It's just that I wasn't expecting it from you," Grace explained.

"Grace, you are my guest," Lao Lao said, "and I want you to enjoy your visit with me. If that means an occasional American breakfast, why not? It's true that I want to teach you some of the Chinese ways, especially since your mother has been lacking in that area."

Grace started to interrupt her, in defense of her mother, but Lao Lao raised her hand to stop her.

"No, Grace. It's the truth. Despite your mother's feelings toward me, I still love her. I will always love her. But trying to deny your own heritage is not acceptable. And not passing it on to your daughter isn't fair to her. You have a right to know your heritage, Grace. What you do with that knowledge is up to you. My hope is that you will embrace your Chinese culture, and blend it with your American experience, in ways that will help you grow. That is all."

Once again, her grandmother had baffled her. She couldn't think of anything to say, so she continued to eat her breakfast in silence.

*****

Since Mr. Liu wasn't coming to pick them up until after lunch, Grace decided to look through Dr. Hall's papers for any information on opium use in China. She found a journal entry from February 1897. Hall had just returned from a conference of missionary groups and native Christians in Tái Yüan Fu, the capital city of Shansi Province. He reopened the hospital on a Sunday and received only two inpatients. On Monday, though, the courtyard was packed with people waiting for his help. He had to turn many away, since he could do nothing for them. Those whom he thought he could help were urged to stay. In the end, he had seventy inpatients, over fifty who stayed in the opium refuge. Hall had a busy schedule. He saw each patient three times a day.

I am also called up at night to see patients who are suffering—suffering untold agony in the effort to leave off the terrible drug. The patients have begged to come, offering to sleep anywhere, if I would give my permission. They are sleeping on the native beds and on the floor, on piles of straw. Fourteen are now sleeping in the chapel on doors and benches. They are eager to leave off the opium so they can plant their crops. I have turned away more than fifty people from the opium refuge, as I could not put them anywhere. They have offered to sleep in the cellar—but this I could not allow. Some of these opium patients are also under treatment for other diseases. (The following Wednesday) My clinics are full . . . between eighty and ninety people were in the court. During the day, eleven carts came, leaving patients. I am very busy, but I am not complaining. We need more help—especially do we pray for a young lady to work with the women. They have no one to visit them regularly, and so much peace and happiness will come to any who will come.

So typical of Dr. Hall to find peace and happiness in treating these opium patients, Grace thought. It wasn't a problem China had with opium in the 1800s; it was an epidemic, and he was in the middle of it. She read Hall used belladonna to help ease them off the drug. But what was opium withdrawal like? A check on her laptop listed both the physical and psychological symptoms of a painful withdrawal that lasted about a week: anxiety, cravings, muscle aches, abdominal pain, chills, fever, hallucinations, nausea, vomiting, diarrhea, fatigue, depression, insomnia, and difficulty concentrating.

That must have been tough, Grace thought. It made her think about Samantha, her college roommate, and she looked up the withdrawal symptoms for amphetamines.

Those symptoms weren't pleasant either: fatigue, increased appetite, twitching, confused thoughts, body aches and pains, unpleasant dreams, emotional outbursts, and depression. The intensity of a person's withdrawal depended on how much they took and for how long. Sam had been using amphetamines for the past year. Grace wished there was something she could do to convince her to stop. Maybe she'd call Sam tonight to see how her friend was doing. Dr. Hall seemed to be growing on her.

As Grace continued her search for Dr. Hall's experience with opium patients, she came across this sad story:

"I want my mother! I want my mother!" The dirty little waif, standing by the roadside, looked the picture of despair. The wind was blowing, oh so cold, and the little five-year-old could, with difficulty, keep its footing. Its outer garment was unbuttoned, and the tapes—mute witness of sex—were loose on its feet. We were near a village. A man came hurriedly round a corner. He was evidently a servant in search of something. Some time passed before he saw the tiny object of his search. He sprang at the child, grasped it by the arm, and, with an oath, walked at a rapid pace toward the village. As he passed our cart, I asked, "your child?"

"No, I have no need for such a little pest."

"It wants its mother. Is she living?"

"Yes, it does, but it will not get her."

The good doctor then pumped the man for information about the child. This is how he translated the child's history: *This child's father is a member of one of the wealthy families of our village. He has taken opium for more than ten years, and all his money is gone. His wife has never taken opium and has always worked hard to keep her children and herself in clothing and food. Just before the last New Year, the man had no money, but he must have opium. He told his wife to dress the two children—he wanted to take them on the street—this girl and a boy three years old. The mother followed them to the door and stood looking after them. Sometime after, she went to her husband's room. He was lying on the kang, smoking opium. She asked for the children. He said do not fear, they will return.*

When the children didn't return, the wife became frantic.

She went on the street asking for the children. She traced them to my master's home. She rushed into the court and into the rooms. Her girl—this girl—was sitting on the floor, crying. She picked her up, started out the door, and almost reached the front gate, when my master came out of his room, struck her and said. "This is my child! I bought it from your husband today for five thousand cash"—and he pushed her out. He closed the door, and the mother started walking to her home, wailing as she went. Someone who knew the circumstances told her, "Your husband sold your little boy to a man from Yang Tsun, and the man took him away in his cart. He got seven ounces of silver for the boy."

Grace was heartbroken. She couldn't get over the cruelty of the man, so addicted to opium that he'd sold his own children in order to buy more. Dr Hall was right. It was a "monster" drug.

The man's money ran out in only a few days, but just before the New Year, he suddenly had plenty of opium again. His wife wondered where he got the money.

The day before the New Year, the husband told his wife to put on her nicest clothing and they would go see the children. She hurried, and they soon entered the court of one of the richest men. The woman said they were in the wrong court, but they went into the rooms occupied by the rich man's wives. The woman went in while the rich man and her husband went on to another room. Soon the rich man came in and the woman asked for her husband. "He has gone home. I bought you from him for ten ounces of opium and thirty thousand cash. You are mine, not his." The woman cried, but that was all she could do.

Dr. Hall had strong feelings about this story:

Sad, sad, indeed! The story is told in a few sentences, but the sorrow and shadow over the life *of that loving mother-heart cannot be expressed in words. And our hearts are saddened when we know that such cases are constantly seen here. It is not uncommon for a man to sell wife and children and home and all for the cursed drug. This province has been the boast of China. But the end is coming. The area planted to opium increases year by year—the users of the vile destroyer are rapidly increasing in number. As opium comes in, peace and plenty and prosperity go out.*

"Not uncommon?" Grace said aloud. How can this be? China was a strange country back then. There are people with drug problems here today, but they'd never be able to sell a wife or a child for it, she thought. She could almost hear Lao Lao reminding her that today's drug addicts cause plenty of harm to their families in other ways. But reading this story in Dr. Hall's journal had Grace wondering, even more, how opium became such an enormous problem in China. She looked forward to talking to Mr. Liu about its history.

* * * * *

After a quick lunch of shredded pork wraps, and noodles with soybean paste—leftovers from last night's supper, which Lao Lao pointed out Grace had missed—she and Lao Lao dressed for their visit to the Lotus Blossom Senior Community in Walnut Creek, fifteen miles away. Grace was surprised by Lao Lao's sophisticated outfit, a pale blue silk-satin dress with short sleeves and a mandarin collar that she called a qipao.

At home, she'd only seen her wearing loose-fitting pants and tops that seldom matched. Grace herself wore a light, yellow, floral, summer dress with spaghetti straps and a shirred waist and top.

As they waited for Mr. Liu, her grandmother explained that it was a Continuing Care Retirement Community or CCRC. She could live independently in an apartment for as long as she was able. If she needed help, she would be provided with assisted living care. Finally, there was nursing care, if she became ill, and memory care. "If I lose my brainpower," as Lao Lao put it. Grace doubted that was likely to happen. Her grandmother was pretty sharp for an 84-year-old woman.

The doorbell rang, announcing Mr. Liu's arrival. He and Lao Lao greeted each other with nods, saying, "Ni hao."

"This is my granddaughter, Grace," her grandmother gestured to her.

Grace had been prepped about the proper greeting. She nodded her head and said, "Nin hao," out of respect for Mr. Liu, who was much older. Mr. Liu nodded and said, "Ni hao."

Grace noticed he was short and slender, although taller than her grandmother. She felt like a giant next to both of them. He wore a neat gray suit with a blue shirt and tie, and carried two cloth bags filled with what looked like Chinese groceries.

"Leave them inside the door for now," Lao Lao said, explaining, "Mr. Liu always brings me special foods from Chinatown when he visits. Thank you, my friend."

"It is my pleasure," he answered, as he gently placed the bags in her hallway.

"Let's go, Albert," Lao Lao said, now that the formalities were over. "Do you know how to get to the Lotus Blossom Senior Community in Walnut Park?"

"I already put it in the Waze, Vivian," he replied, as he offered his hand to help her down the steps.

Grace was startled to hear him use her grandmother's first name. She'd never thought of her as anything but a grandmother. She followed them to Mr. Liu's car, an older Ford Focus that was well kept and clean.

On the way to Walnut Park, Lao Lao and Mr. Liu sat in the front seat and kept up a steady conversation in Chinese, with an occasional foray into English when they wanted to include Grace, who was seated in the back. She was wondering if she'd ever get the chance to talk to him about the history of opium.

When they arrived at Lotus Blossom, the manager gave them a tour of the six-story building, ending at the apartment that would be Lao Lao's. It had an empty living/dining room, a small kitchenette, and a bedroom to the right with a bathroom and a large closet. There was also a small balcony accessible through sliding doors beside the kitchen. Not much color, Grace thought, but she was sure Lao Lao would fix that problem. Mr. Liu took out a metal measuring tape, the kind that contractors carried, and began to measure the different rooms, writing the results in a small notebook. Lao Lao frowned and whispered something to him.

Grace wondered what was wrong. The place seemed to have everything that Lao Lao would need: a spacious garden area, three meals a day in a formal dining room, in-house laundry and dry cleaning, a resident beautician, plenty of activities, and stores within walking distance. They even had a kind of living room area on each floor where residents could relax and visit each other.

In the car on the way home, Lao Lao and Mr. Liu continued to talk in Chinese. This time, it seemed as if she was arguing with him, and he was trying to pacify her. What was going on? Grace wondered. The argument continued at home, while Mr. Liu carried his two bags into the kitchen with Lao Lao following. Then, silence. Mr. Liu carried a bottle of wine with two glasses across the hallway, past Grace, and into the dining room.

"As a guest, I'm usually given the place of honor," he said, as he sat in the chair which was facing the door and on the far side of the enormous table with a window behind him. He filled both glasses with wine. "Would you care to join me, Grace? I poured the other one for you." He smiled and handed her a glass.

"Thank you, Uncle," she said, accepting the wine. "I'd love to." Although Mr. Liu was only a good friend of her grandmother, Lao Lao had told her to call him "uncle." She said it was the proper way to address older Chinese people. Mr. Liu seemed pleased. At least she got that right. But where should she sit at a table that seated eight? She decided to sit two chairs to his left and in front of the China cabinet. As she sat on the chair's woven dragon, she thought, *I hope it won't bring me bad luck.*

"Good choice," Mr. Liu said, a twinkle in his eye. "I

understand you want to talk to me about some Chinese history."

"Yes, I do," Grace replied, taking a sip of wine. "I've been reading the journals of this medical missionary who worked in China from 1896 on. He wrote about the opium problem then. Do you think you could explain the history leading up to it and why it was such a huge problem?"

"I'd be happy to," he said. "Opium has a long history, I'm afraid. It was originally found in an area of the world now called Turkey. Opium, as you probably know, is an extract from the poppy plant which grew there. It was first brought to China, probably in the early 600s by Arabs and Turks, and it was taken orally, as a medicine to relieve pain. It wasn't until smoking tobacco was introduced to China, around the 1600s, that smoking cocaine became a problem. Although there were a couple of attempts by the Qing Dynasty during the 1700s to prohibit the sale and use of opium, they were unsuccessful."

"Why was that?" Grace asked.

"Partly because of outside influences." He removed his glasses and cleaned them with a cloth from his pocket. "You see, the Portuguese first found they could make a handsome profit by selling opium to the Chinese. Then, the British East India Company discovered an inexpensive and abundant method to grow poppies in India, and they became the major suppliers of opium to China. Soon, other western countries joined in, even the United States. Since China had a ban on the opium trade, the drug was brought in by 'private traders' who sold it to smugglers along the China coast. Of course, the money always found its way back to the East India Company or other western companies."

"The opium was smuggled in? That's outrageous."

"Also, there was a trade issue," Mr. Liu added.

"I don't understand," Grace said.

Mr. Liu explained, as he put his glasses back on. "England had a trade imbalance with China, Grace. Imported silks, Chinese tea, and porcelain pottery found a strong market in England. But the Chinese didn't want anything that the British manufactured. Importing opium to China fixed the imbalance. Opium was something the Chinese wanted."

Grace shook her head. "That doesn't sound very nice."

"It got even worse," he said, sipping his wine. "The amount of opium imported to China increased from two hundred chests annually in the early 1700s to forty thousand chests a year by the mid-1800s. Opium use continued to grow until it became an economic and social concern. When the Qing Dynasty in China tried to destroy the imported opium and stop its trade during the 1800s, Britain went to war with the Chinese—twice. You may have heard of the Opium Wars?"

Grace nodded.

"Well, the Chinese lost both of them. The first war kept the Chinese from stopping the opium trade and gave Britain even more trade rights. It also handed Hong Kong over to the British. The second war actually legalized the opium trade. By the end of the war, as many as sixty thousand chests were imported each year. And it just kept growing from that."

"So even though the Chinese tried to stop opium from

coming in, they couldn't. In other words, it wasn't all their fault," Grace exclaimed.

"Well, they weren't completely innocent. After all, they *were* using it. By the time the Chinese were able to stop the trade of opium a few decades later, they had another problem. The Chinese had become successful at growing their own opium poppies. It wasn't until the Chinese communist government took over in 1949 that the habit of smoking opium was wiped out. Actually, it took another few years, until 1959, to eradicate it completely."

"You know that missionary doctor whose experiences I'm reading about?"

"Yes, the one you mentioned earlier." Mr. Liu took another sip of his wine.

"I wonder if he realized how much England and his own country had done to make matters even worse for the Chinese," Grace said.

"Probably not," Mr. Liu answered. "It's unfortunate, but most people don't pay attention to history the way it actually plays out. We have a tendency to justify our own side, whether or not we genuinely understand what we're justifying."

Just then, Lao Lao burst into the room with a tray filled with Chinese food and delicacies, which she firmly set down on the center of the table. "You can't change my mind, Albert. I'm not moving!"

Oh no, thought Grace. *So that's what the argument was about. What next?*

7

"It's Only a Girl"

Lao Lao didn't want to move to the Lotus Blossom Senior Community because the apartment they showed her was too small to hold all the furniture she wanted to bring. *Was she crazy?* thought Grace, who believed the plan all along was to sell or donate her Chinese furniture so she could move to a smaller place. Had she planned to bring it all with her? Was that why she wasn't in a hurry to make a list where everything should go?

After a delicious dinner and more arguing, Mr. Liu had finally thrown up his hands. "I give up," he said. "You're impossible, Vivian!" And stormed out. Poor Mr. Liu. He was only trying to help.

Grace and Lao Lao cleared the table and cleaned up the dishes without a word. Lao Lao wasn't talking, and Grace didn't know what to say. Later that evening, Grace called her mother and unloaded on her. All she got was, "I told you what she's like. Why do you think I moved to the other side of the country?" Grace could see she was going to have to handle this problem on her own.

The next morning at breakfast, Grace got more of the silent treatment. She was starting to feel very alone. After the brief talk with her mother last night, she'd called both Samantha and Adam. Neither one had answered. Grace decided to see if she could find refuge in Dr. Hall's papers.

After thumbing through his journals back in her bedroom, she noticed a story about a little girl who was ill. Some of her previous reading had implied that girls and women were treated like second-class citizens or worse during the 1800s. She wanted to know what that meant. She decided to read, lying down on her bed and propping her head up with a pillow. What was it like to grow up as a girl back then? This was what she learned:

"Not important! Not important! It's only a girl! It's only a girl!" The man had come to me for medicine for his child.

When Dr. Hall suggested it would be easier to treat the child if he brought her to the hospital, the man had shouted those words. He lived ten miles away, apparently too far to bother with a girl. It seemed the Chinese had different attitudes toward children at birth. A boy was considered *"Heaven's choicest blessing,"* while a girl was a sign of *"Heaven's displeasure."* According to Dr. Hall, a girl's life was far from pleasant.

I can see so little in the lives of these dear little ones that could be called happiness or even comfort. When a girl baby comes to a home, no demonstration is made—the father is considered unfortunate, the mother unlucky. Poor little waif! Not a word of welcome, not a loving caress—except by the poor mother. Mother-love seems to exist the world over. If the family is large or if the older children are girls, the little visitor does not remain long. The nurse either strangles it at once, or it is cast aside to die. Wrapped in a bundle of hay, it is carried on to the wall, if in a city, and dropped over—if in a village, it is carried outside the village. This is done at night. You will ask, "what becomes of the bodies?" Ah, the wolves and the dogs make short work of all that is given them. The bundle is quietly torn open and the little one is no more! These little piles of straw are everywhere visible.

Dr. Hall was quick to say that girls were not "despised" in every family. Some families were happy to have girls. But the life of a Chinese girl who was allowed to live, was no picnic.

Soon, we see a plump, happy baby—they walk and talk early—and, after a fashion, can play around the room or in the court. For three years, all may go well—then comes to the little life something over which it has no control—the mother does not let it go barefoot. With strong, cotton tape, the little feet are bound—beginning at the toes, the tape is wound around, up to the ankle. These tapes are gradually tightened. The little body increases in size—the little feet cannot. By the tenth year, the feet are usually out of shape—the toes are doubled and pressed together; the heel is elevated by means of small round blocks of wood, the weight of the body is on the toes and the ball of the foot—and a life of misery is the result. The bones of the feet are crushed, bent, or broken. The smaller the foot, the more fashionable! I have seen little girls five or six years old, sitting on the ground or on the doorstep, who would be continually putting the hands to the feet—they would cry and sometimes try to loosen the bandages, but to no avail. The little hands would stroke the aching, throbbing feet, while the eyes—mute witnesses of the unspeakable agony—would fill with tears. The faces often assume an habitual expression of suffering. Now the little one cannot run and play. She can only hobble around— she must rest every few minutes—she must not complain, she dare not alter her condition. When she attains the age of twelve to fourteen years, she is betrothed to some man she has never seen.

Grace had been wondering about the loose tapes on that five-year-old girl's feet, the one whose father had sold her for opium. But forcing a child to "hobble" around and selling her into marriage at such a young age? Did Chinese girls manage to get any control over their lives back then? She was afraid she knew the answer. Could a girl's life in China have changed so significantly in a hundred twenty years?

Not far away is a district where it is the custom to betroth a girl to a boy many years younger than herself. There may be frequently seen girls with boys on their backs (their future husbands) and these boy-husbands are veritable tyrants in their treatment of their future brides. A boy of six, bound to a girl of ten, seems to try every possible method of torture in his efforts to keep her mindful of the fact that she is his personal property. He will beat her in the face, spit in her face, pull her hair, throw dirt in her food, kick her, revile her and make her carry him from place to place, when he wants to change his location. She often is installed as nurse-girl for her husband. She makes her boy-husband's food, puts him to bed at night, dresses him in the morning and is at his beck and call all the time. She must (even) carry him when he does not want to walk. She does not dare raise a word of protest, for that would bring swift punishment from her mother-in-law. She has now become the personal property of her husband's mother—and that mother can make her miserable if she chooses to do so. So long as this mother lives, the daughter-in-law must serve her. The girl who goes to school or is taught lessons in language is the rare exception.

In other words, Grace thought, she was like a prisoner, completely without freedom. Grace was curious to learn more about a Chinese mother-in-law. After flipping through the pages of Hall's journal, she found one. It was a story of a nineteen-year-old mother whose baby was about two years old. Her young husband had brought her to the hospital for treatment.

The woman was suffering from a disease which yielded readily to treatment. She was bright and quick to learn, anxious to be taught, and seemed interested in the Gospel. She manifested great affection for her little one and, when her husband came, they seemed a happy family.

A few months later, Dr. Hall was called to the woman's court to see an old patient who had returned. It was the same woman. Her father had carried the suffering woman from the cart to her room. Moaning from pain, she told this story:

She returned to her home, happy in her restoration to health. She could help with the work and divide the cares of the humble household. She was well, and so all looked bright. But she had incurred the enmity and displeasure of her husband's mother—her owner. The mother-in-law said she was well now, and she would always be running about. She was better sick, for then she could not leave the room. The taskmaster began to prove her power. Her tongue was harder to bear than her tasks. At length, she began on the husband. Why had he taken his wife away from home for a month? Why had he proven so ungrateful to his old mother? The best thing he could do was to beat his wife—that would make her good!

"And just see this baby. Its mother has been sitting around, talking and eating, and has neglected the child. Beat her, beat her! You won't beat her! You dare speak thus to your mother! Undutiful son!"

Then she went into a (convenient) fit and announced that she would put an end to all this trouble, and to her life at the same time. They then began pleading with her, but to no avail. There was only one way to avert her death—if the son would beat his wife with her (the mother's) stick, she would be his mother still. Otherwise . . .

The man, to save his mother's life, took up the stick and began beating his wife. He beat her over the head and shoulders, until she fell over on her face, then on the back and limbs, until his mother came out of her "fit" and told him she was satisfied. The girl was unable to rise, and she pleaded to come to Li Man to the doctor. The mother would not let her come—she kept her in sight to better vent her spleen.

It was only when the husband had to go back to work in a distant town that the mother realized she would have to nurse his wife. Instead, she had her son load his wife into a cart and take her to her parents, who had brought their daughter to the hospital.

Her body is beaten black and blue—the tears come, and you can see her hands clench from the pain when she moves. I have made the poor aching body as comfortable as I can and will do all that is possible to remove from her body all evidence of this,

one of China's darkest, most hopeless customs—the
tyrannical rule of the mother-in-law.

Grace put down the journal and wiped the tears from
her eyes. Was it because she was a woman, a partly Chinese
woman, that the story affected her so much? The part about the
mother-in-law had made her angry. But Dr. Hall's description
of the poor woman's body, and the way he tried to make her
comfortable—that's what brought her to tears. He had every
reason to be angry at the way his patient had been treated, but
he seemed more saddened by the unfair custom of mother-in-
law rule. Meanwhile, his primary focus was on caring for his
patient and treating her with kindness and respect. Grace was
touched by that.

She was still angry, though. That husband could have
beaten his wife to death if the mother-in-law hadn't stopped
him in time. Dr. Hall wrote that many women, especially the
poor ones, had ended their lives because of a mean mother-in-
law. He wasn't referring to all Chinese mothers-in-law. Some
were kind and gentle and loving. There were other troubles,
though, that caused young women to escape by ending their
lives. Dr. Hall told the story of one woman who saw no other
way out.

*This woman was twenty-eight years old—
attractive and intelligent. Her husband had been dead
eight years. He was sixty, she fifteen, when they were
married. For five years, she roasted his opium and held
his pipe—a slave rather than a wife. That she should
have acquired a taste for the drug is but natural. For*

nine years, she used it regularly. The family heard of our ability to free opium slaves, and she came to us gladly. She heard the gospel daily—how much she understood and accepted we can never know. Let the assistant speak.

She returned to her home, strong—the longing for opium was all gone. All the family were pleased with her. Two weeks after she returned, her husband's brother announced that he had sold her to a rich man in the city. This man had four or five wives, but they all took opium, and he needed someone to wait on him. The poor woman said she would not go. She had served one man and had been a slave for thirteen years. She was a slave no longer, and she would remain free. The man tried to force her to do his bidding and, at last, she told him she would die first. The woman told him it was not right for the old man to have so many wives—the True God said so. Today, she was to go to her slavery again, but she went to her death instead.

The woman had died from an overdose of opium. It had been deliberate. Although the assistant had attempted to save her, he was unable.

Poor woman! She preferred death to such a life. Her death will pass unnoticed. There will be one mouth less for her husband's brother to feed. Had she lived and refused to obey the man's order, her life would have been one continuous round of abuse, and *she would have been subject to many wrongs. Had she entered the rich man's home, she would soon have been a slave, a double slave again. Did she choose the better portion?*

Grace stopped when she read the last part. How unusual for this man, a doctor and a missionary, to ask that question. Wasn't suicide supposed to be a sin in the Christian faith? Weren't doctors all about saving lives, against all odds, not losing them? Yet, Hall had such sympathy for this woman's life struggles that he couldn't condemn her for leaving them behind. It was almost as if he understood her, Grace thought. What an extraordinary man.

A beep from her phone pulled Grace out of her musing. It was Adam.

"Sorry. Missed your call," he texted.

"Why didn't you call me back? I miss your voice," Grace answered.

"Busy, babe," he texted. "Moved in with a couple of guys."

"Where?" she asked.

"Summer rental on Long Beach Island."

"Having fun?" she asked, wishing she were doing the same.

"Sorta," he wrote.

"Meaning what?"

"Got a part-time summer job. Bar tending. Good money," he answered.

Adam was all about making money. His plan was to work some day with his dad, a private equity investor. He'd applied for an internship this summer at Blackstone, but they'd turned him down. He wasn't surprised. Blackstone got thousands of applications. Grace thought he'd decided to take the summer off.

"That's nice," she said.

"You bet. Live off half. Invest the rest."

"Sorry?"

"Roommate likes to day trade. Learning myself," Adam explained.

"Make any money, yet?" Grace asked.

"Gotta go, babe. Time for work. See ya." And that was it.

Grace was frustrated. What good was having a boyfriend if he didn't act like one? She wanted to share her experiences with him. Then again, how could she? Grace had always cut a part of herself off from other people, including Adam. Now she was living with her Chinese grandmother and reading about a man who went to China years ago as a missionary and doctor. If she talked about what she was doing, it wouldn't take Adam long to find out she was Chinese herself. Lao Lao had said it was important to understand her culture. Maybe it was time to tell him the truth. Didn't she trust him? What was holding her back? What was she so afraid of?

* * * * *

Lunch consisted of sliced pork meat in a sweet bean sauce wrapped in pancakes, which Grace was able to eat with her hands. Lao Lao was speaking again. It was as if the argument with Mr. Liu had never happened.

"How was your reading today?" her grandmother asked.

"I read about how girls were raised in China back then," Grace replied.

"Ah, yes. How they bound their feet. It was difficult for children and women, and I'm happy people no longer do it."

"That wasn't all, Lao Lao. Did you know that many families left their daughters to die, just because they were girls?" Grace stared hard at her grandmother, wondering what her excuse would be for that particular custom.

"It sounds as if your Dr. Hall worked with poor and uneducated peasants. Educated people and people with wealth did not act in such a way. They knew which customs were acceptable and which were not."

"That doesn't make it right, Lao Lao," she argued. "Did your educated people make any effort to stop these simple people from murdering their own children?"

"China is a complicated country, Grace." Lao Lao laid down her chopsticks. "Back then—even now—the population was too great to accomplish such an undertaking. It was best to accept the way poor people thought and to move on. Did your Dr. Hall find it easy to bring his Christian ideas to China? I think not."

"You're right, Lao Lao. He did find it difficult." Grace stood as if to make her point. "He also found it difficult to treat patients who were afraid of cleanliness and fresh air, the necessary requirements for healing. But he kept at it, all the same. Do you know why? Because he cared about his patients. Despite the fact that China had an enormous population, despite some of the crazy things they did, he wanted to help them. Do you know how many patients he helped just in his first year at Li Man? He treated one thousand eight hundred sixty-eight cases. These people weren't just from Li Man. They also came from villages that were miles away."

After a moment, Lao Lao spoke. "You seem to be very impressed by your Dr. Hall."

Grace answered, "He's your Dr. Hall, too, Lao Lao. He came from America to help your people. And you know what? He made a deep impression. Because of Dr. Hall, not to mention all the other medical missionaries who came to China back then, the ideas of western medicine were introduced to your country . . . our country." It was the first time Grace had thought of herself as Chinese.

"You're right, Grace," Lao Lao said, with a puzzling smile. "People like Dr. Hall made a big difference in our country. I'm happy that you're reading his journals. You have learned much, and you will be able to teach me, and my Chinese friends, what you have learned."

It was a response that Grace wasn't expecting.

"I have something else to tell you now," Lao Lao went on. "We will be going out to dinner tonight. My dear friend, Evelyn Chen, has a grandson whose name is David. He's a third-year student at Stanford University Medical School. I told Evelyn that you may be interested in medicine, and she thought it would be good for you to talk to David."

"Lao Lao!" Grace burst out. "Is this a set-up?" She admired her grandmother's ability to change direction in a conversation with such ease and speed.

"Of course not, Grace." Lao Lao acted as if she were

offended. "I would never do that to my only granddaughter. I will be there, also, to help guide your conversation."

"Why? Doesn't this David speak English?"

"Of course he does. I just thought you'd need help dating a Chinese man. Have you ever dated one before?"

"First of all, 'dated?' Second, no I've never dated a Chinese man. Wait! His name is David. Isn't he American?"

"Yes, Grace," her grandmother replied patiently. "He's a Chinese American, born in the good old USA."

"Then why do I need you to guide our conversation?" Grace asked.

"You're right," Lao Lao said. "You don't need me. Good. I'll stay home. I have much to do tonight. David's coming to pick you up at six pm sharp. And wear something dressy. I hear he has expensive tastes in restaurants." With that, her grandmother swept out of the room.

"Wait . . . where are you going?" Grace realized she'd been had by a clever 84-year-old woman.

8

The Good, the Bad, and the Ugly

eading about the brutal lives of girls and women in China had disturbed Grace so much, she decided to take a break from Dr. Hall's journals. She was curious to see what else might lie in the trunk, so she went back to the small room off Lao Lao's bedroom. She noticed a second trunk, similar to the one she'd opened a few days ago.

Inside the trunk, she found pieces of fabric, carefully folded. She carried several of them into her bedroom and unfolded them, one by one, on her bed. She couldn't believe what she saw. The first two articles were colorful Chinese tapestries with embroidered pieces attached to silk backgrounds.

"Those are from the Qing Dynasty," said Lao Lao, who had just entered the room. "It was the last dynasty of China, and it ended in 1912. That is when your Dr. Hall was in China, I believe."

"These are amazing," Grace said. "And they all seem to be made from silk."

Lao Lao smiled. "Did you know that the making of silk was invented in ancient China? It dates back to the fourth century, B.C. and is made from the cocoons of silkworms who feast on mulberry leaves. The cocoons are softened by boiling and the fiber from the resulting ball is spun into silk threads. At first, fabrics made from silk were worn by only the emperors of China. Over time, its use spread throughout Asia and then to other parts of the world. You must have heard of the Silk Road, Grace."

"Yes," Grace answered. "It was a trade route between China and Europe."

Her grandmother nodded her approval. "It was called the Silk Road because silk was in so much demand. Also, silk fabric was used by Chinese for writing because it absorbed ink well. Today, China is the largest producer of silk in the world."

"That's amazing," Grace said. "Is it used for anything else?"

"Good question," Lao Lao replied. "The silk cocoons are also used to make silk comforters. Instead of turning the fiber into threads, they gradually stretch it into a kind of flat web, the size wanted for the comforter, and keep adding layers. Although silk comforters are lightweight, they're very warm. The comforter on your bed is made from layers of silk floss, covered with a cotton cover, and then placed inside a silk duvet cover."

"I was surprised at how warm my comforter was," Grace admitted. "But these tapestries are unusual. And the workmanship is incredible."

"Also, embroidery is one of China's great arts. This one is very delicate." Lao Lao pointed at a long wall hanging with different widths of long strips of silk sewn together, a creamy white strip at the top, a slightly wider turquoise strip with silk embroidered flowers below that, and a much wider, salmon-colored strip, with a silk embroidered assortment of people walking or riding different animals, in various hues of blue, green, purple, and rose. The last strip was finished with an embroidered design that matched its hues. The entire piece was bordered on three sides with a plain black silk strip, with tassels made from the silk threads embroidered on the inside.

"It's so intricate," said Grace. "Even the details of the faces are embroidered. I would love to hang it in this room, but I think it may belong in a museum."

"Do you see these stitches that look like a tiny circle with a dimple in the center?" her grandmother asked. "That is called the forbidden stitch."

"Why?"

"Some believe it was forbidden because women often went blind while working with these embroidery stitches. That certainly could have happened, but I think there's another reason."

"What is it?"

"For hundreds of years, the winter home for the emperors of the last two dynasties was in a large compound in Beijing. It was called the 'Forbidden City,' because most people weren't allowed in. The emperor and his household lived there, and it was the center of Chinese politics. The 'forbidden stitch' was supposed to be used only in clothing for the emperor and his family."

"How big is the Forbidden City?"

"Within its walls are many gardens, temples, and palaces," her grandmother said. "I believe there are almost one thousand buildings. It has an outer court and an inner court, several gates, and it covers about one hundred seventy-five acres. Now it's a museum, of course. Tourists to and from China visit there every day."

Grace opened up the last folded piece, which took her breath away. It was a man's robe, made from a rich, slate-blue silk, with dozens of off-white and beige flowers and butterflies embroidered all over it. The neck, sleeves, and bottom had a wide black border with more intricate stitching. The embroidery was made with silver and gold silk threads, which gave it a luminous quality.

"Do you think Dr. Hall wore this robe?" Lao Lao asked.

"I . . . I guess so," Grace answered. She felt as if she were holding history in her hands.

Lao Lao stood up. "I have something to show you," she said and left the room. A moment later, she was back, holding some photographs in her hand. "I found these when I brought you the other writings. I didn't know if you wanted to see them." She handed them to Grace.

The pictures were in sepia. The first one was of a tall man with a dark beard and long dark moustache, definitely not Chinese. He wore a dark mandarin jacket with very wide sleeves that reached to his lower hip. Beneath it was a quilted gown with narrower sleeves that hung several inches longer than the ones on his jacket. They were so long that you couldn't see his hands.

"Do you think that is Dr. Hall?" Lao Lao asked.

"I guess so. I mean, who else could it be?" Grace replied.

"That's a kind of mandarin hat he's wearing," her grandmother said. "They are made in six pieces. Sometimes it's called a six-piece-hat."

Grace turned to the next picture. It appeared to be the same man with a woman and two children, a boy and a girl. They were all dressed the way an American family would at the time. "Wait. This is a family picture. Dr. Hall had his family with him in China? How did I miss that?" As she turned to the third picture, which was of a woman, Grace said, "And this must be a portrait of his wife."

Lao Lao looked at her. "Does he not mention his family anywhere in his journal?"

"Not that I've noticed so far," Grace said. "There's still a lot I haven't read yet."

"Why don't you go through a few more entries," Lao Lao suggested, "while I return these silk pieces to the trunk for safety."

Grace searched through the journals, until she found a trip Hall's family took, which involved having a mid-day meal at a Chinese inn.

The accommodations in a Chinese inn must be seen to be appreciated. The one we occupied, six of us, was about ten by twelve feet, and nearly one half of this was taken up by the kang, or bed. The room was without fire. A table, which must depend on the wall for uprightness, and one chair, minus one leg, was all the furniture the room contained. A man soon appeared with a pot of boiling water and three bowls. These he placed on the table and, when he had asked us what we would eat, went out to prepare our food. Altho we usually carry our own food, it is not considered respectful to enter an inn without eating some of their food. The food we received was reasonably clean, and I presume it would be palatable to a hungry man. Mrs. Hall has not taken kindly to chopsticks, so she carries her knife, fork, and spoon. Carl and Enid and I do use chopsticks, tho,' I confess, we do not use them with becoming grace.

Aha, Grace thought. Dr. Hall had a boy and a girl, just as his photograph indicated. And Mrs. Hall didn't know how to use chopsticks either! She must tell Lao Lao. Wait. Something was off. Dr. Hall wrote that there were *"six of us."* The Halls were a family of four. Were there more children? Or maybe a nursemaid? At the end of another journal entry, she found a partial answer. Dr. Hall had written about another child.

Our baby, Lois, has been very ill. Day and night have we watched her, and the dear Lord has given her to us, for a comfort. We are thankful to him for His mercy.

That brings the number of family up to five, Grace thought. From what Hall had written, it sounded as if little Lois had recovered from her illness. It looked as if the family photo had been taken in the state of Washington. It probably was just before the family traveled to China, and maybe Lois was born there. Grace felt as if she were putting together the pieces of a puzzle. But for now, she enjoyed reading the rest of Dr. Hall's description of the inn.

Outside the door, our mules and horses are eating. Flies have taken full and complete possession of both inn and manger. Amused smiles play around the faces of the wondering natives, who crowd as close as possible to the door, hoping to get a sight of foreigners 'taking food.' The bottom of the door is a foot from the ground and the dogs crawl under to inspect our food. Paper windowpanes come full of holes when wet fingers are applied, and eyes show at every little tear made by eager men and women and boys who stop at nothing to get a glimpse of us. Start toward the door and they scatter like pigeons, only to return when the coast is clear.

Grace loved Dr. Hall's humorous description of the curious Chinese, who may never have seen white people before. But his description of the inn where they spent the second night of their journey was far from amusing . . . at first.

We stopped at night at a most miserable place. The inn had neither broom nor chair, hot water nor fire. The room assigned to us had never been swept since the building was erected. The door had no lock—the latch was broken off, the lower hinge was twisted, and the door squeaked every time it was moved either by one of us or by the wind. A cat and four kittens lay asleep on the "kang." Some millet hay was piled up in one corner and an old rush mat was spread over part of the bed. Cobwebs galore swung from dirty black rafters and scorpions played hide-and-seek in the holes in the walls.

By now, Grace had seen the word "kang" several times, so she turned on her laptop and checked the online dictionary. She learned that a kang was a brick or clay platform built across one side of a room, warmed by a fire underneath and used for sleeping. They were common in northern China's houses. This one didn't sound comfortable, though, especially since it had no fire for warmth. And six of them sleeping on it together? Grace had difficulty picturing the properly dressed Mrs. Hall spending the night at that inn. According to Dr. Hall, it was a miserable time, at least for him.

By the time our meal was ready, we were too tired to eat. The children were put to bed on some of the quilts we had brought from home. Soon they were fast asleep—all cares forgotten. All our belongings were piled in heaps around the dirty room. Sleep seemed out of the question, but exhaustion, at last, brought oblivion, and we managed to become unconscious for a time.

All night long men were coming and going in the inn (with) loud voices, raised in angry controversy. The dirt bed was hard. Turning from side to side, I spent a good part of the night trying to find a soft spot. The bed was so short, I could not stretch myself and my covering was so narrow I could not wrap myself in it. A dog tried to cuddle up to my back and tried to bite me when I objected.

The mother cat had to sing to her babes every few minutes and appeared to be running a free lunch counter at all hours. Fleas began a base-ball game on my back and everyone seemed to be at bat all the time.

Mosquitos took possession of the place. Patriarchs and plebeians, young men and maidens, were singing their maddening song of blood and destruction, and every unprotected spot of human flesh was made an instant target for unnumbered sharpened knives and bayonets. Hard blows, self-inflicted, helped to torture the flesh . . . and not a blow, to my knowledge, landed on a single mosquito.

A mule broke loose somewhere in the yard and went from stall to stall, foraging and blowing dust from his nostrils. He tried to work the pump and overturned the water-trough. He got his head through the door of the room next to ours. There, he found some bits of hay and grain. Grind, grind, blow, blow, paw, paw, make the door go squeak, squeak. Oh, it was maddening!

An owl flew up on top of the inn and began shivering out his old, old question. I wanted to tell him 'who' but had no strength to rise.

The wind was blowing. Door-screens scraped against the walls. Loose tiles on the roof jumped up and down and made a little pat-pat noise.

I turned over and lay on the cat. She spat fire at me and said all the mean cat-words she could think of, and then I jumped up and pitched her out the window. That is, I tried to pitch her out, but just as she left my hand, she turned and caught her claws in my loose outer garment, and in me, and clung for dear life. When I got her loose, she started down my body, head up, cutting my flesh with every step she made.

Nineteen roosters entered a tournament, and all were out to win. The one nearest my head would flop his wings four or five times before trying out his voice and after his attempt he would clear his throat with a little sucking sort of whistle that almost made one commit murder or suicide.

Venders of dried meats and fish and fruits called out their wares in tones that pierced the brain. Visions of weird animals, made up into convenient packages for hand management, appeared to vex the tired minds. Hungry mules, flying through a firmament made up of swords and bayonets and angry cat-voices, made one feel sure they were resting quietly and serenely in the nest of the dragon.

Oh dear, is it possible that it is time to get up and start on our journey? Yes, the headman of the inn is calling his guests and there's no more time for unhappy dreaming.

Poor Dr. Hall, Grace thought, but she couldn't stop laughing as irritation after irritation kept piling up during that unforgettable night. It was his fault for being such an entertaining writer. Fortunately, the good doctor had a pleasant ending to his trip.

We came to a little inn by the roadside about the middle of the day. Everything was clean. The man in charge wore a white apron. We called for a meal, and it was served without noise. There were onions and beans and bean sprouts and bean curd, and garlic and steamed bread and meat with gravy, and rice and pears and sweets, all served outside under a mat canopy. This made us forget the nightmare of the last night and we were happy again.

Grace was relieved to learn that Hall's journey with his family had ended on a positive note. But she'd gotten so caught up in his latest journey, she'd forgotten to tell her grandmother what she'd learned about Dr. Hall's family.

"Lao Lao!" she called out.

A moment later, her grandmother returned to her room, clutching something in her hand. "What is it, Grace? Did you find out about the doctor's family?"

Grace explained what she'd learned, then added, "You know, Lao Lao, I thought it was amazing that Dr. Hall was able to go through what he experienced and still keep a positive attitude. But he had his whole family with him. How difficult that must have been, not just for him, but for his wife and children. Can you imagine having a baby in a foreign country, and one that was as backward as China was then?"

"At least her husband was a doctor," Lao Lao said.

"That's true, I guess, but it still had to be stressful."

"Sometimes life can be stressful in this country, too, Grace. Raising a child without a husband is not easy. Especially when that child fights you all the time." Lao Lao sat on her bed and looked up at her.

Grace placed her hand gently on her grandmother's shoulder. "I'm sorry that you and my mother don't get along," she said, relieved that Lao Lao didn't push her away. "It wasn't easy for Mom, either. Especially after she lost her father. She said it changed her in a big way."

"Yes, I know," her grandmother answered with a sigh. "She changed from a girl I knew to . . . I don't know . . . somebody I couldn't find, no matter how hard I tried."

"Maybe neither one of you was to blame. You missed your husband, and she was angry that all her Chinese 'good luck' superstitions had failed her. Didn't my grandfather die at the beginning of the New Year?"

A look of understanding gradually came over Lao Lao's face. "Of course. That's why she was so angry all the time."

"I don't think she was angry with you," Grace said. "I think she was angry at her culture for lying to her. But you haven't stopped loving your culture. It's a part of you. I think that's why she pushed you away." Grace took a chance and gave her grandmother a quick hug. Lao Lao didn't stop her.

Then her grandmother jumped up. "Talking about stress. You have only one hour to get ready for your date with David Chen." She opened her hand, which was holding a beautiful jade necklace. "I want you to have this. Maybe you have something to wear with it tonight?"

"Oh, Lao Lao. Thank you. It's beautiful." She held it up to her neck. "I have the perfect dress to go with it. Are you sure you don't want to go with us?"

"With David Chen?" She pretended to be shocked. "I never date younger men!"

9

MEN AND BOYS

race was surprised when David Chen appeared at Lao Lao's door. He was much taller than she'd expected. He was also better looking, which left her feeling a bit flustered.

"You must be Grace." He looked down at her with a smile. "It's great to meet you, finally."

"David?" she said, looking up at him. He had warm, brown, almond-shaped eyes and short, dark hair. He was wearing a navy blazer and light blue, striped shirt with gray pants and black loafers.

"You weren't expecting me to be this tall, were you?" He was grinning.

"No. I. It's just that . . ." stammered Grace. She tried not to blush.

"It's okay. I'm used to it. The men from Northern China are usually taller than the ones from the South. Plus, I was born in California, so all that healthy American living added another couple of inches. I'm really not that tall. Five-foot-ten in my stocking feet."

"Ni Hao, David," Lao Lao said, appearing out of nowhere.

"Nin Hao, Auntie," David answered her, and he bent down to give her a kiss on the cheek.

Lao Lao looked pleased. "And how is my smart, handsome doctor doing?"

"So far so good, Auntie," David answered. "I passed the first step of my board exams."

"Of course you did," Lao Lao said. "What are you doing this summer?"

"I'm shadowing my pediatrician since I may go into that line of medicine. Pediatrics will be one of my rotations this year and I want to get a good feel for it."

"You will make a wonderful pediatrician, David. You've always had a good way with children." Lao Lao patted him on the shoulder. "Enough interrogation. You and Grace need to hurry if you want to make your reservation. Are you taking her to Eight Tables?"

"Not this time, Auntie," he said. "I thought she might be tired of Chinese food after staying with you for several days. We're going to Chez Panisse instead, not the dining room but the café upstairs. It will give us more time to get to know each other." He looked at Grace. "Are you ready?"

"Uh . . . yes . . . I," she mumbled. Her head was spinning. What did he mean by, "not this time" and "It's great to meet you finally?" Before she knew what was happening, David had taken her by the arm and whirled her down the steps and into his red sports car.

"I don't want you to get the wrong idea," he said. "I'm not a playboy. It's a Pontiac Fiero, and it's very, *very* used."

Grace laughed. "What a relief," she said.

* * * * *

They sat opposite each other in the café at Chez Panisse, as the waiter wrote down their selections. Grace ordered the butternut squash ravioli with brown butter, sage, and parmesan. David chose the oven-braised lamb with celery root puree, chard, and chanterelle mushrooms. He'd also ordered a lovely bottle of red wine they both enjoyed. They'd made small talk in the car on their way to the restaurant, but Grace was curious about David's familiar tone.

"I get the impression you know a lot about me," she said.

"I do . . . in a way." he replied. "I know that you only met your grandmother once, but your mother sent her a school picture of you every year. You could say I watched you grow up. You could also say I've watched your mind grow up, too. Your mother sent copies of every story and essay you ever wrote. You have a lot of writing talent, Grace."

"I don't understand."

"My grandmother, Evelyn Chen, and your grandmother have been best friends most of their lives," he explained. "They share everything with each other. In fact, they've been planning to set us up for years now."

"I'm so embarrassed," Grace said, blushing. "I didn't know." David smiled back. What a nice smile, she thought.

"Don't be," he said. "I wasn't waiting around for you. I've had a few girlfriends in the past."

"I'm glad," Grace said, with relief. "I didn't even know you existed . . . until now."

"Well, I sure knew you existed." David laughed, then became serious. "I hear you've been reading the journals of some American doctor who worked in China during the late 1800s and early 1900s. It must be fascinating."

"It is. I had no idea the problems that existed in China back then," Grace said, glad the topic of conversation had turned from her. "His name was Doctor Hall. He was a medical missionary, and he lived there with his entire family. You can't imagine the struggles they had to put up with."

"China was a backward country then," said David.

"In more than one way. He lived in a village in Shansi Province and wrote about everything he saw. The opium epidemic, the superstitions people had, their brutal ideas of medical practice, their lack of cleanliness, not to mention the way girls and women were mistreated."

"You mean the way they bandaged girls' feet so they could hardly walk?" David asked.

"It was worse than that," Grace explained. "Baby girls were not welcomed in many families. They were often killed at birth or thrown away for the wolves to eat. Any girl who was lucky enough to live had her feet bound at the age of three and was sold into marriage when she reached her early teens. She had no choice in the matter. After she left her family, she belonged to her mother-in-law and husband. Some people treated these girls like slaves and were unbelievably cruel."

"I had no idea it was that bad. What about the boys and men in China?" David asked.

"I still have to find out what Dr. Hall says about that." Grace answered. "But from what I've read so far, having a boy seemed to be considered a blessing, while having a girl was considered bad luck."

"Seems like Dr. Hall didn't find anything good about China back then," David said.

"I guess it sounds like that," Grace admitted, "but he

actually cared about the people he treated. And he respected them. He was also a missionary, you know, and he believed that teaching them about Christianity would help to solve many of their problems."

"Did it work?"

"Not really," Grace conceded. "The Chinese people were suspicious of him because he was a foreigner. They thought foreigners were only interested in taking control of China. Not surprising, after the way they were treated by the British."

"The Opium Wars?" David asked.

"Yes. Anyway, I did research and discovered that only a small percentage of Chinese people were Christian today, although the number seems to be growing."

"Our family has been Christian for quite a while, probably thanks to the missionaries who came to China back then," David said. "But we were an upper class, educated Chinese family. It looks as if Dr. Hall was living with the poor, illiterate Chinese, who lived in the rural areas."

"True. But I don't think it's fair to turn your nose down at people who don't know any better. Why did it take a man like Dr. Hall, who came from a different country, to help those poor, uneducated people in China?" She glared at him.

David's expression turned thoughtful. "Of course, the usual answer to your question is that China is a large and complicated country. It was too big a problem to solve—especially for the relatively small number of educated elites."

"That's what Lao Lao said." Grace leaned toward him and raised her hands. "But that's no . . ."

"I'm not finished, Grace."

She sat back, dropped one hand on the table, took a sip of wine, and waited.

"You're right. It's not a good excuse." David seemed a bit agitated. "And it takes people like your Dr. Hall to show us that it's worth the effort, no matter how difficult. I agree with him. The lives of all people should be respected." David reached for her hand as if to make a point. "That's why I want to be a doctor, Grace. I'm not doing it to make a lot of money. I want to be like Dr. Hall. I want to treat people who really need my help, whether it's children or old people, or . . . " He pulled his hand back from hers, a little embarrassed by his enthusiasm. "Yeah. I've never told anyone that before."

Grace was touched, but concerned. "David, medical school is so expensive. How will you pay back. . ."

"I'm fortunate. My grandmother is paying for it. She sold real estate in San Francisco and did well. She's been putting money away for my education for years." He smiled that nice smile again. "There's something else I want to do, and my grandmother agrees. These days, doctors in China believe there's value in traditional Chinese medicine or TCM. Even doctors in this country have started to combine the ideas of Western and Eastern medicine in their treatments. I'd like to do the same."

"You want to study acupuncture, too?" Grace was impressed by this forward-looking young man.

"Not exactly. I wouldn't perform acupuncture myself, but I'd like to learn more about it. That way I'll be able to send my patients to a competent, certified acupuncturist, if I believe their situation warrants it. My 84-year-old grandmother practices Tai Chi, you know. It's helped with her balance, arthritis, and back pain. Even taking herbs can be helpful, as long as they come from a doctor who understands them well."

Grace hesitated. "What I've read about TCM indicates that acupuncture and Tai Chi are relatively safe," she said. "But taking herbs can be dangerous."

"Agreed," David replied. "That's why I'd be careful to find a certified doctor who really knows about herbs," he said in a serious tone, "It's also important that western medicine should take priority.

Grace looked at him. "Not to change the subject, did you know that Chinese doctors in the 1800s pushed long iron and silver needles right through the areas of people's bodies they believed were diseased? They thought they were getting rid of the bad spirits who had put sickness there."

David looked shocked. "Did you learn that from Dr. Hall?" he asked.

"He witnessed it on more than one occasion," Grace answered. "His descriptions are pretty vivid."

"I didn't know that," David said. "I'm glad TCM has improved since then. I'd love to read what he wrote about it."

"David, you said your grandmother is paying for your medical school. But what about this?" She looked around her. "I know this restaurant isn't cheap. How can you afford it?"

"My grandmother gives me a small monthly allowance, too. Medical school keeps me busy. I don't have much time to spend it. So, I save it up for special occasions like this."

"I'm sorry. I didn't mean to be rude," she lowered her

eyes. What was it about this guy that made her so outspoken? "Sorry."

"It's okay. You don't know me . . . yet." She could feel him staring at her. "By the way, I like your necklace. Did your grandmother give it to you?"

"Yes," she said, looking down and fingering it.

"A beautiful necklace for a beautiful woman."

Grace raised her eyes to meet his gaze. Damn, she thought. There's that smile again.

* * * * *

The next morning at breakfast, Lao Lao grilled Grace about her date with David. She wanted to know every detail: What did she think of Chez Panisse? What did they eat? What did they talk about? What did she think of David?

"Enough, Lao Lao," she said at last. "I had a good time, and I don't want to talk about it anymore."

"Of course, Grace," Lao Lao said, an apologetic tone in her voice. "I won't ask any more questions. Your love life is none of my business."

"Love life?" Grace jumped up and cleared her dishes. "All I did was go on a pleasant date with a nice guy, and now you're talking about my love life?" She didn't tell her grandmother about the text she'd gotten from David last night, saying he hoped they could get together again soon. Or the fact that he'd kissed her at the door, then apologized for being so forward. But she'd liked it. Still, there was Adam to think about. She had to admit, however, that David seemed more thoughtful and attentive.

Anyway, today was a new day, and she'd promised David to make copies of Dr. Hall's writing about the Chinese doctors. He was showing more interest in Dr. Hall than Adam had. Of course, it wasn't Adam's fault. He didn't know about Dr. Hall or Lao Lao or the fact that Grace was half Chinese. Maybe it was time to tell him everything.

But first she wanted to look up what Dr. Hall had to say about boys growing up in China. She flipped through pages until she came to that part. It was right after the section on girls.

How different when a son is born! A son is important! He must be cared for, and his slightest wish is law. He must be protected from disease and from the myriad evil spirits which exist. Some friend of the family, "locks him to life." This ceremonial I do not know—but I have seen some very dirty strings and bands and metal strips around the necks of some of my little patients. I am told that the article is fastened on to remain until the child's twelfth birthday! The condition of the amulet is not important—the intention is all important. Nothing would induce a parent to remove the charm for an instant. (Meanwhile) Holes are made in little girl's ears soon after birth—girls, babies, women and grandmothers wear earrings. Girls are "not important," The spirits do not trouble girls. They want boys! I have seen baby boys with a ring in one ear. This is to deceive the evil spirits who want boys. The spirit, on seeing the earring, immediately decides that the owner is a girl! And the spirit wants boys! The spirits (also) fear tigers, so the caps made for little boys are made to resemble a tiger. With ferocious head and mouth and tail, the tiger is always on guard. The child can play or do anything he wishes—the tiger protects him!

The boy's slightest wish is law? No wonder those Chinese men thought they could do whatever they wanted, Grace realized. They learned it as boys! But Dr. Hall had more to say about boys.

The boys are taught to gamble from babyhood. I am told that the general idea is that by teaching a boy to gamble; he is made shrewd and more able to look out for himself. Go where you will. If you find boys, you will find gambling. One day I watched two little boys, aged 5 and 7 years. Each had four or five copper cash. They cast lots to see which should play first—they wagered one cash on which side would turn up when a cash was pitched up in the air. They put down a cash and pitched other cash at it—the nearest won. They fought and quarreled over their decisions and at last, after spitting at each other, each little gambler went his own way—looking back only to heap imprecations on the other's head and accuse him of dishonesty.

Ha! thought Grace. It seems all they learned was not to trust one another. What could you expect from two little boys, each of whom had been raised to believe he was perfect?

At five or six, a boy is sent to school. He's not an ideal student at all times, but some of the customs of the school are worthy of note. The boys all study at the top of their voices. The din would seem to me almost unbearable. I did not know, until a day or two since, the real motive for this screaming (as I call it). I was talking with the teacher at our school in the city. The schoolboys were studying as loud as possible. Some were lying on their beds, some standing in the door, others sitting on stones in the court, and yet others walking around—but each boy had his book, and each seemed to want to raise his voice highest. I remarked that we did not have that custom in America, that each boy studies to himself. A man standing by said, "How do you know when the boys are deceiving you? If we hear their noise, we know they are getting their lessons. If our boys are quiet, we know they are not studying."

A boy goes to school when he arises in the morning, and his task is ended when it is so dark he cannot see. He has a short time for his meal at noon, and a few minutes at other times for rest, but he is expected to put in all his time at his work. This is only an expectation, for they seem to go about as they please. If the teacher is an opium user, the boys are sometimes said to supply him opium so he can sleep, and they can play.

Deception seemed to be a major issue here, whether it was the two boys who were gambling or the students who had to study in loud voices to prove that they were actually studying. Of course, if I had to study from dawn until dark every day, I might try to get away with something, Grace supposed. But boys providing opium to their teacher? Then, in another part of his journal, Dr. Hall told the story of two boys from a different perspective.

Two little boys, nine or ten years old, were standing at the front gate when I went out this forenoon. They were in rags. One had a small basket, and each carried a little bag. The thermometer stood at about 20°, plus the wind was blowing. I asked what they were doing. "Looking (through) ashes for bits of coal." I told them to come in and took them to a pile of ashes from the stove in the chapel. They could not believe me when I said they might pick the ashes. But I convinced them at last and then those cold, dirty fingers fairly flew in and out and thru that pile of ashes. The bodies shivered, and the rags danced in the wind, and as I stood near talking to them, their little tongues were loosened and told me many things of the emptiness and desolateness of their lives. Time after time, they went thru the ashes, and when they were ready to go, all that remained was barely enough to mark the spot.

That was Dr. Hall in a nutshell. One minute he made you angry and frustrated at the way people are acting, and the next minute he's breaking your heart with a story of two poverty-stricken children who just wanted a little heat on a cold day.

Grace wiped a tear from her eye as the phone rang. It was David.

"Hi, Grace," he said. "I hope I'm not calling at a bad time. I was interested in what you told me about Dr. Hall last night. I wanted to see if you learned anything else today."

"I just finished, David," she said. "I'll read it to you." Grace proceeded to read from Dr. Hall's journal about boys: being able to do what they want, as if it were law; being taught to gamble so they can become shrewd; and going to school from daybreak to dark, yelling their lessons to prove they're studying, and giving opium to their teacher so they can play.

"It's no wonder girls had such a hard time back then," David said. "The men must've had egos that wouldn't quit. Not that it was perfect for women in this country. They had to fight for a lot of rights during the 1900s. The situation still isn't great. The female students in our school have to work twice as hard as the male students. A lot of the guys think they're better because they're men. Someone's always making a comment about women not being strong enough or tough enough to perform some of the work we're asked to do. The only time I saw a med student faint, it was a guy."

"Now I want you to hear the last story Dr. Hall told," Grace said, and she read him the story about the two boys looking through the ashes for bits of coal.

"Wow. I don't know what to say. I guess I have a lot to live up to," David said.

Grace heard herself say, "So do I."

"Look, Grace," David hesitated. "I didn't just call to find out about Dr. Hall. I really enjoyed being with you last night and . . . Damn. Look, I have to go. Dr. Bentley needs me. I'll call you later if that's okay."

"Sure," said Grace, her heart racing a little. "Bye."

10

A Marriage Proposal

Lao Lao walked into Grace's room when she got off the phone with David. "Talking to a boyfriend back home, Grace?"

"No, Lao Lao," Grace said, not offering any more information.

"Talking to David, maybe?"

"Lao Lao!" Her voice went up a few decibels.

"Never mind. Not important. I wanted to tell you that my book club ladies are meeting tomorrow night. We would like for you to join us. We'll be discussing a book by Amy Tan, called *The Joy Luck Club*. Have you read it?"

"No, I haven't, Lao Lao," Grace answered.

"Maybe you saw the movie?" her grandmother asked.

"I don't think so."

"Ai, I keep forgetting how young you are." Lao Lao shook her head. "In that case, you will benefit from our conversation. Here is my copy of the book, in case you want to read it before our discussion," she said, handing a worn copy to Grace. "Or maybe you will choose to read it afterwards. It is our custom to discuss the book while eating dinner together. Tomorrow night at 6 p.m. Don't forget." She started to leave, then turned back. "I'll bring you some snacks to satisfy your appetite before dinner."

Grace sighed and tossed the book on her bed. She wasn't

looking forward to an evening with Lao Lao's book club ladies. Especially if they were going to discuss a book she hadn't even heard of. She'd been planning to bring up the idea of her grandmother moving to the senior community, but she wasn't sure how it would go over. Maybe she should wait until after the book club meeting. One way or another, she knew she'd have a fight on her hands.

She opened a page in Dr. Hall's journal and came across a letter he wrote in April of 1897. A quick glance indicated that the journal entry was about the differing customs between getting married in China as opposed to America. He seemed to have written it in the form of a dialogue.

"Doctor, I have heard that in your country, the men ask the women to marry them. Is it true or not?"
"That is our usual custom."

"Did you say to Mrs. Hall 'will you marry me?' and did she reply, 'yes, Dr. Hall, I will? And were you all alone? And did you drink tea together before you asked her? And did your 'middle-man' hear you ask her and hear her answer?"

I answered the last question by saying, "We do not require a middle-man in America."

"But who guarantees your wife if you do not have a middleman? How do you know what she can do? Did you see any of her work before you asked her? Could she do her food and sew and make shoes? How did you know she did not take opium?"

"I had eaten food prepared by her. I knew she could sew, but I did not once think of asking her if she could make shoes."

I should say here by way of explanation that "making shoes" should be called "The Old Man of the Sea" to Chinese women. Wherever and whenever you go, you will see young women and old—stitch! stitch! stitching away—making shoes. From childhood to dotage, the weary round goes on. In season and out of season may be seen the moving thread, thro and thro, back and forth, with incessant and unvaried monotony. Her own tiny shoes must be made at spare moments and in the secrecy of her own room. But the husband and the father and the sons must have shoes, and the women must have them ready when called for. If more shoes can be made than present necessity requires, the shops will take them to sell to their customers.

All common shoes are made of cloth—tops, sides, soles, and all. The sides of the shoes are usually of new cloth—may be cheapest blue cloth or finest velvet—but anything will do for the inside of the thick soles. These are made by pasting together several thicknesses of material. The outside is covered with new cloth and the whole mass is then sewed together. The soles may be from one-fourth inch to two inches thick and the shoes—as I find them—are most uncomfortable. The toes *are pressed together, and the heel slips up and down in a most provoking manner. I think, sometimes, the Chinese would be more enterprising in a different foot gear. I know I would.*

So, on top of having to cook, sew, and serve their husbands, Chinese women had to make their shoes and keep them in shoes, whenever needed. Hers were not considered a necessity. She had to admit, though, that even today many women in this country held down jobs and took care of the home and children. Grace wondered what Dr. Hall would learn about the differences in finding women for marriage in China.

I said, "Mr. Wang, did you ask your wife to marry you?"

"Me? No! She had nothing to do with it. All she had to do was to get married."

"How long did you know your wife before you were married?"

"What do you mean? I did not know her at all. Why should I trouble myself about that? The affair was managed by the middleman. I was at home at my work. You see, I did not have so much bother to get my wife as you did to get yours!"

"How did you manage the affair to get your wife?"

"I engaged the middleman to find me a wife and told him how much I could spend for a wife and—"

"Oh, I see. You told the middleman what kind of a wife you wanted; that she must be such-and-such, an age and clever and—"

"No! Of course, I did not! If I should do all this, what need would I have for a middleman? I told him I wanted a wife; it was his affair to find her."

"How did he manage to find her?"

"I do not know. He found her and I had no cause to ask questions."

"But I want to know how he found her."

"Why? Do you want another wife?"

"No! I want to know your custom, that is all."

"I do not know the custom in other villages, but the middleman must announce that he wants a wife for such-and-such a man; she must be able to work, must be born on a lucky day, must be good-looking and must be able to show some of her work. She must be of a different family and must furnish her own bedding."

"Did you see her before you were married?"

"Yes, I saw her once, after the affair was settled."

"Did you discuss the matter?"

"No, I did not speak to her. That would have been indelicate."

Indelicate? Ha! Grace suspected that Dr. Hall had enjoyed this conversation about finding a wife. The Chinese were serious about their marriage contracts, though. Once completed, they couldn't be dissolved. He gave a couple of examples. First, he told the story of a beautiful girl who lived in this village and was engaged to a wealthy man who had offered more money for her than anyone else.

She had nothing to say about the plan for her future. She was not permitted to speak to her intended husband before marriage—and she could not after the ceremony. Not until after she was taken to his home, did she know that her husband was a mute. He was deaf and dumb—had never heard a sound or spoken a word in his life! The girl died last June—but not until she had borne four children to her husband—the two older like the father, the third like herself—the baby four days old when the cord of life was broken, and a life of untold misery and sadness was at an end forever.

The second story was to show how someone's death could affect a marriage.

Two years ago, in this village, a man died a short time before the date set for the marriage ceremony. Did his death release the girl? No! At the appointed time, she was united to his spirit and is now his widow. A dummy, or image, was used to represent the man—this image was carried in the chair in the wedding procession that the dead man would have occupied had he been living. The girl followed after, in her chair, arrayed in the garments of a bride. Some part of the ceremony was at the grave—she was united to each of his three spirits (or souls) and must go through life with this relationship. I have not heard a more pathetic story. I find so much sadness in the lives of these women. They are only women and being women, they can only accept a woman's portion.

Born to lives of sadness and misery and physical suffering, having no pleasure in this life or hope for the life to come, it does not surprise one when they find oblivion through opium. I asked one poor, pitiful woman why she did not let her baby daughter live. She replied, "I could not let it live for even two days, when I knew what was before it, if its lot in life was as its mother's."

Reading these stories broke Grace's heart. What impossible lives these poor women had lived as a result of a superstitious, backward, patriarchal society. How she wished she could have improved their lives. It reassured her that Dr. Hall and Mrs. Hall were able to find such joy in the work they did.

We have now more than thirty women in the hospital. I see them and hear their stories of suffering and loneliness and hopelessness every day. Pain, pain, pain! Here, there and everywhere. Their lot in life most sad; their lives so dreary and monotonous! Two have not walked for years. They sit from day to day, with folded hands and saddened faces, looking forward to death and—what? We have no one (foreigner) to speak to them. Mrs. Hall goes to them every Sunday and every second day during the week. She is doing all she can for them, but her family requires much at her hands. If you could see the happy faces made so by a kind word, a flower, or a bit of dainty food, you would not need to be told why Mrs. Hall is so happy in China or why God has blessed us both by bringing us to this place.

Grace didn't know what was happening to her. She felt as if these women, who lived over a hundred years ago, belonged to her. For years, her mother had encouraged her to hide the fact that she was half Chinese. But now she wondered if her mother was justified in denying her a legacy. She thought about her roommate Sam, and the way she talked about her life and family back in Jamaica. Sam loved her darker-skinned cousins and enjoyed their company. It's true that she took advantage of her light skin at school. But it was different from the way Grace hid the fact that she was Chinese. Sam knew her family. Grace didn't know her family at all. She was surprised to learn that her stubborn grandmother was growing on her. Mr. Albert Liu was so charming. And David Chen was a sweet, curious, thoughtful man.

She made up her mind. It was time to call Adam. Not text him. Call him. And tell him the truth about her. She was about to grab her cell phone when it rang. It was her roommate, Sam.

"Sorry I didn't call you earlier, Gracie," Samantha said. "I didn't get back from my little vacation until today."

"Vacation?" Grace wondered. "You didn't say you planned a . . . where did you go?"

"Might as well tell you the truth," she said. "You've been nagging me about it all year."

"Nagging you?" Grace was confused.

"Detox, Gracie, detox! I finally went, right after school got out."

"Thank god, Sam," she said, with a feeling of relief. "I've been so worried about you, ever since I read about the opium epidemic in China, back in the late 1900s."

"What opium epidemic?" Sam asked.

"I'll tell you all about it later. But what made you do it? The detox, I mean."

"It wasn't exactly my decision," Sam admitted. "My mother found the pills I was taking and had a convulsion. She threw everything into the toilet and flushed it away. It wasn't a pretty sight."

"Was it difficult, Sam?" Grace asked. "I read it was difficult."

"When did you start reading about the symptoms of detoxing?" Sam asked. "Yeah, it was difficult. But I'm over it now. I'm a new woman."

"Detox is nothing to joke about, Sam. It's important for you to stay clean."

"I know, I know. So, when are you coming home?"

"I don't know," she answered. "My grandmother has decided she doesn't want to move after all. But she's eighty-four. She can't live on her own forever. I've got to convince Lao Lao to change her mind."

"Who's Lao Lao?"

"That's the Chinese name for your grandmother on your mother's side."

"I need you, Gracie," Sam whined. "I'm taking a summer class to improve my writing skills for when I have to write my Senior Honors Thesis this year. I'm not as good a writer as you are. You need to edit my work."

Grace laughed. "It doesn't have to be done in person. Email your work to me, and I'll send you back my edits."

"Have you heard about Adam?"

"Heard what?" Grace's heart skipped a beat.

"He's got a bar tending job on Long Beach Island."

"He already told me. He's making money to pay his rent and invest with some new friend," Grace said.

"Typical Adam," Sam snorted. "It's all about money with him."

"Don't start, Sam."

"I never liked him, Gracie. He's a cold fish. He doesn't have the kind of warm spirit you deserve."

"He's not very romantic," Grace admitted. "But he's a decent person. Anyway, I was just about to call him when you rang. I plan to tell him the truth about me."

"Good luck with that." Sam said. "Gotta go. I have a Narcotics Anonymous meeting in twenty minutes. Promised my mom I'd go this summer."

The two friends said goodbye, but before Grace had a chance to call Adam, Lao Lao entered the room.

"David called," she announced. "He said your line was busy. He wants to come by later, around 7 p.m., so he can make copies of what Dr. Hall said about Chinese doctors. He knows I don't have a printer."

"That's fine," Grace said. "I have all the papers ready for him. I thought it was better to make a copy. I don't want to lose the original."

"Also, it's nice you get a chance to see him again." Before Grace could respond, Lao Lao exited the room.

Grace called Adam, but he didn't answer. She left a brief message, asking him to call back when he was free. She was still feeling emotional from Dr. Hall's stories about how women were treated in China. For now, she chose to read something lighter. She found the letter where Dr. Hall talked about going to a large fair in his village and bringing along an imaginary "foreign" friend. In one section, Hall bargained with a man selling baskets.

"What is your price on this basket?"

"You want to buy that basket?"

"I do, if your price is what I think it should be."

"My prices are always what they should be. I would not dare deceive you. It is impossible for me to ask too much for a thing."

"How much?"

He took the basket, turned it over and over, said something in an undertone to his associates, then turning to me said, "I will sell you that basket for two hundred and twenty cash."

"You flatter me. That cash for this small basket?"

"I do not make a cash on it at that price and will not sell for less."

"I will give you one hundred cash."

"Very small, very small. Say you will give more. I will take just two hundred."

"And I will give one twenty."

"Less than two hundred cash will not make a sale."

"More than one hundred and forty will not make a sale. You see this basket is small. It is not smooth on the inside, and, in fact, I do not care whether I buy." I turn and say, "We will go."

"Give him one sixty. Give him more."

This from a by-stander who always takes it on himself to help out a bargain.

"Come on, we will not buy today. We will go to some other stall."

"Come! Come! Sold, sold! One forty."

This call comes as we start away. We return, pay for our purchase, and the man is just as eager to begin another bargain. This must be tiring, you say? It is, but there is no way out of it. Everything we buy to *eat, wear, or look at must be bought in just this way. The natives all do it so, and it would never do to pay what is asked. I tried it once when buying some eggs. I asked the man his price. He knew what we had been paying, but he named a figure about one-third higher. I accepted his offer. He looked up quickly into my face and said, "You did not hear correctly. Eggs are expensive today. That amount will not buy them." He named a higher rate. I turned away, and he called out to me to return. The fault was his and he would take the regular rate.*

Grace laughed. She knew bargaining was common in other countries, but she'd never had the nerve to do it herself. Her mother teased her about it when they traveled abroad. Her mom was a natural bargainer. Maybe she couldn't escape everything about being Chinese. Dr. Hall said that bargaining was hard work, but it gave him the opportunity to learn the language of the people. Then he described one more odd custom.

Suppose I want to buy a pound of fat. The price is one hundred cash. I say "I want fifty pounds. What will you want?"

"If you want so much as that, you will have to pay more. I will sell you fifty pounds at one fifteen."

Grace hoped that the farm people and peasants who lived far from the cities had improved their math skills by now. Finally, Dr. Hall took his imaginary friend to the cloth shops at the fair.

Come inside this tent. Oh, how beautiful you say? Yes, rather bright to our foreign eyes, but the natives delight in bright colors. This clothing is ready made. See these heavy silk garments. They are wadded with cotton for winter wear. The natives try to keep warm by piling on clothing rather than by fires. The summer garments are delightful—see this white silk. You wonder why I do not buy such? I have not yet seen but one ready-made garment I could wear. I am so tall and so large that all my garments must be made to order. Some very old garments are beautiful. They show wonderful work, and some are seen with pictures worked in silk, illustrating some old Chinese legend.

Like the beautiful clothes I found in your trunk, Grace thought. Once again, Dr. Hall had charmed her with his delightful sense of humor. Lao Lao had conned her into reading his letters in the first place, but now she was hooked. She'd learned so much about life in China back then. She felt as if she owed the good doctor for sharing his unusual experiences with her. It didn't seem fair that she was the only one fortunate enough to read about his life and work. It should be shared with the world.

* * * * *

That evening after dinner, David stopped by for Dr. Hall's letters about Chinese doctors. He asked if she wanted to go with him. She did, but she was waiting for Adam to call back, and her talk with him needed to be private. Grace could tell David was disappointed. She was surprised to realize she was disappointed herself.

"Tomorrow is Saturday," he said. "Your grandmother says you haven't been out of the house much. I have the day off. Maybe I could bring back Dr. Hall's original letters tomorrow afternoon, and we could take a walk along the waterfront." He gave her a hopeful look.

"I'd love to go with you, David," Grace said, as she watched his earnest look turn into a warm smile.

"Great! See you at one!"

David turned and ran down the steps, as if he were afraid she'd change her mind.

"Why didn't you go with him?" Lao Lao once again appeared out of nowhere.

Grace turned to her grandmother and smiled. "Because I have a book to read for tomorrow. After all, I don't want to disappoint your book club ladies."

11

The Book Club Ladies

Hdam never called, and Grace got halfway through *The Joy Luck Club* before she fell asleep. The book was about the relationships between four Chinese women who immigrated to America in the 1940s and their American-born daughters. It mirrored much of what happened to Lao Lao and her mother. Grace hoped it would help her to understand their broken relationship.

After breakfast, Grace tried to call Adam again with no luck. David wasn't coming by until 1 p.m., so she decided to read a bit more of Dr. Hall's writings. Maybe she could share some of what she'd read with the ladies tonight. After all, it was a similar topic. This time, Grace focused on a story he'd titled, "Six Thousand a Year—Plus Rice."

He has an income of six thousand a year—plus rice. He has, also, tuberculosis of the hip-joint, and walks with a crutch. His body is twisted, and only his eyes appear normal. The regular charge in the dispensary, for out-patients, is fifty cash per month. Then, in addition, each one pays ten cash a day for the dressings. One day, he came into my office and told me he could not come again. He could not afford to pay so much for the treatments, so would have to stay away. The thought of staying away made him weep, and his weeping touched my heart. An order was issued admitting him to the dressing-room without further expense. He works outside the dispensary door—perhaps a hundred feet from my front gate. He is seldom away from his stool. Once I called him into my study and asked for a history of his life.

Dr. Hall wrote that the man was so grateful, he told him every last detail he could recall. Here is what he said:

I am twenty-eight years old—and half a year more. I was born up there in the hills, five miles from where we sit. There are about thirty families in the village. They are rice-farmers and laborers. My family owns nearly two acres of land, but more than half of it is occupied by graves. They have owned the land since the Ming dynasty. The graves must have proper care, and I must go home twice a year to worship before the grave of my father. Should I neglect this important duty, some great infirmity might be laid on my body. I am afraid not to go. My father died when I was eight years old. He was just like I am now—only more so. He was so stooped that he could not look straight out but had to turn his body and look side-ways. He coughed all the time.

Grace read that two of the man's brothers and three of his sisters had died as babies. His mother wasn't sick, and he had one surviving sister who had two sickly children of her own.

I cannot understand why my people should get all this sickness. At my home, the door is always closed at night and the window is both closed and covered with a garment. It does not seem possible for any sickness or evil spirit to get inside the house. My sister will not even let her children get out in the air. She wants them to be healthy and strong. She keeps the baby wrapped up all the time. The air has never touched her. O no, she would not dare touch water to her body. I do not understand why she is so weak.

The poor man, Grace thought. He was afraid of the very elements that would have helped him. The man couldn't remember when he first became ill, but it got worse when his father died.

That year my legs hurt all the time, and a doctor stuck needles into them. Then they hurt worse than before, and the swelling of my hips was greater. I took many kinds of medicines from many doctors, but the swelling grew larger all the time. One day, it opened a hole, and the pus came out. My mother called two doctors. They said I must not let the poison out, so they fastened the hole up with plasters. When it began to leak, they piled on more plasters, until I was almost covered with them. When the plasters dropped off, I felt better. When they closed the opening in my leg, I got a sickness all over and felt hot all the time.

I was never able to work in the rice-paddy. Whenever I got my feet wet, the cough came on and my hips pained harder. When I was twelve years old, my mother brought me to the city and signed me with this man here.

It was sad how the man had suffered from treatments by his Chinese doctors. Everything they did made his situation worse. Dr. Hall must have been appalled by his story. Added to that, the man had been working for the same master for sixteen years. For the past eight years, he had made six thousand a year—plus rice. But his latest term was up, and his master had cut him down to half-rice. That meant he had to pay for half his food. It was why he couldn't afford to pay for his treatments.

I work all day long; except for the few minutes I take to come to the hospital for my treatments. I go to work when the daylight is almost the same as the night, and I stay at my work as long as I can see the hole I make with my awl. After it gets too dark to work the thread thru the shoe sole, I put my work away until tomorrow. After work, I sit in the door and watch the people pass along. Sometimes there is music in the inn opposite, and I can hear that without spending any money. I never leave the city, excepting on the two days I go home to worship. On those days,

I start for my home when the birds begin to sing, and the dark is over everything when I return. I walk not very fast and stop to rest quite often. All these years, I have been making soles for shoes. I first paste the bits of cloth together, and then put on the skin bottoms. I can almost make soles with my eyes closed. I have been sitting on that stool, where you see me working every time you pass, since I came to the city the first time. I sleep on the floor just inside the front door of the shop. After the door is closed for the night, I spread my bed on the dirt floor. I can almost stretch my feet out straight, but not quite. I usually feel better when I can have my feet propped up on the box in the corner. Then my thighs do not feel so tight.

I do not think I shall ever take a wife. Wives cost so much, to begin with, and I could not support a wife as she should be treated. I know a wife would be always wanting to spend money, and that would not be right. Then, again, I have no place to keep a wife if I had one. She could not stay here. The gods have laid a curse on me, and I shall die without having a son to worship at my grave. That is very bad.

I give my mother four thousand a year out of my earnings. That helps to pay for her food. That leaves me two thousand a year for myself. This suit of clothes will not last longer than one more year. Then I shall have to spend more money for clothes. There is always something to take the money away after it has been earned.

Last year my master gave me a whole silver dollar when he paid my wages. That was the first dollar I have ever owned, and I took it home to my mother. She is keeping it to pay for candles to burn at her funeral. She wants to be buried as nicely as any of her neighbors.

The master says I am getting nearly three dollars and a half (if it was paid in silver) for my work each year, and he thinks that is too much. He says he wants to find someone who will take my place and work cheaper. If he finds one to take my work away from me, I do not know what I shall do.

In your honorable country, do you have many men who earn six thousand a year—plus rice?

NOTE: *Six thousand copper cash per year equals two dollars, gold.*

It was a long story, but it spoke to Grace in so many ways. The poverty, the ignorance, the sickness, the pretense at healing, the superstitions, the simple desire to share his life with someone, family duty, the wish to help his mother despite his illness and poverty, and Dr. Hall's need to record his story. It was all there.

* * * * *

"Are we still on for today?" David asked when she opened the front door at 1 p.m.

"Absolutely," Grace answered. "I could use a little sunshine right now." She had tried calling Adam again, and still, he didn't answer. At least David wanted to be with her. She was looking forward to spending the afternoon with him.

"Why don't we drive over to the Golden Gate Park in San Francisco," David said. "There's a Japanese Tea House and Garden I think you'd enjoy. We can get a cup of tea and walk around the gardens. I like to come here when I need some peace and quiet."

"It sounds perfect," Grace said.

Neither of them spoke on the drive over. It didn't seem necessary. David had a music CD playing softly, and he turned to smile at her a couple of times. Grace closed her eyes and nearly fell asleep from the sweet sound of music, combined with the hypnotic hum of the wheels on the road.

David bought them each a cup of tea. Then, they walked around the gardens, delighting in the peaceful waterfalls surrounded by colorful azaleas, lilac-blue wisteria, and green dwarf trees, as well as the rich red of the Japanese maples. He threw a small throw blanket on the grass for them to sit and reflect on the lovely surroundings.

Grace took a deep breath. "It smells so sweet and fragrant here. I wish I could take it home with me."

"I knew you'd like it." David said. "Is it okay if I take a picture of you with the flowers in the background?"

Grace laughed. "Haven't you seen enough pictures of me already?"

"This one is for you," he said, as he snapped a picture with his phone. "As a memory of your time here."

"Then I think it should be a picture of both of us," Grace answered. "Here. I'll take it." She pulled out her phone and leaned her body toward him. "There. Now we can both have a memory."

"How much longer will you be staying?" David asked.

"I don't know. I was planning on moving my grandmother into her new home, but now she's fighting it. There's also the problem of Dr. Hall's letters. She wants me to return them to his family, but it doesn't seem enough."

"You're thinking they belong in a museum?"

"Yes, but a museum still doesn't seem to be enough," she answered. "The hangings and clothing will be perfect for a museum because people can admire them as a whole. But you can't just look at Dr. Hall's writings. They need to be read."

"So, they need to be in a book?"

"I guess," she replied. "But how can it be done? The subjects are not in any particular order. Some of them were written as Dr. Hall experienced them. Others are stories that seem to stand by themselves. Besides the stories I've told you about, there's one about Buddha that includes many of his teachings, and another about an actor-philosopher named Ma Lo-Ling who describes the seven torments of hell. There are also a couple of operas, and a list of a hundred Chinese proverbs. To add to all that, Dr. Hall was in China for over twenty years. Most of what I've read so far takes place in the first few years."

"Why don't you write about it?" David suggested.

"Me?" Grace was startled by the idea.

"Sure. You're a terrific writer. At least you were in high school. You could write about how you discovered Dr. Hall's writings, include some of them in the book, and add your own point of view as a Chinese American."

Grace shook her head. "But I've never written a book before."

"There's a first time for everything, Grace."

"To be honest, David," she offered a guilty look, "I've never thought of myself as a Chinese American."

"You clearly don't look it, but the fact is you are," David said with a gentle tone. "Maybe it's time to accept the culture you came from."

"I don't know if I'm ready to do that." Grace looked him in the eyes and let him see her fear.

"You don't have to make up your mind today." He smiled and took her hand. "You don't have to make up your mind, ever."

His smile was so kind, so welcoming, that she knew she could trust him.

"Thank you, David," she said, and leaned over to kiss his cheek.

David's smile got wider. "A kiss from the most beautiful girl I've ever met! I'm one lucky guy!"

"Flattery will get you everywhere," she teased.

"But right now, I need to get you back home, so you can meet the amazing book club ladies."

* * * * *

At home, Grace returned to her room to pick up her copy of *The Joy Luck Club* and some of Dr. Hall's letters. Her grandmother already had an impressive spread of Chinese food set on her dining room table. She heard the doorbell ring with the first of the ladies arriving, but decided to call Adam one more time. This time she reached him.

"Adam, I've been calling you for ages. Why didn't you get back to me?" she said.

"I've been busy, Grace. I'm not your lap dog, you know," he answered.

Wow. That was rude. She decided to ignore it. "I know you're busy, but I had something important to tell you."

"So, tell me. I don't have all day," he said, then she heard him call out to someone else, "Pass me the chips, babe."

"I'm sorry," Grace said. "Are you with someone?"

"I'm with a lotta people, Gracie. Geez, you're possessive. What am I supposed to do with you in California? Become a recluse?" She heard someone laughing in the background.

"No, it's just that I . . ." Grace hesitated.

Adam snorted. "Look, if you have something to say—say it."

"I don't know if this is the best time," she said. "Maybe we could talk later when you're alone."

"Sure, whatever, bye." Adam hung up.

Grace looked at her phone. After his rudeness, she should be angry or upset or something. Instead, she felt relieved. Why was that?

Her grandmother called from the dining room. "Grace, all the ladies are here! Are you coming to join us?"

Grace picked up the book and letters and made her way to the dining room. There were four other short, elderly Chinese women with wrinkled faces, sitting with Lao Lao around the table. Three of them had gray hair and one was dyed blond. It seemed as if they were all talking in Chinese at the same time.

"Ladies," Lao Lao rapped on the table until they were all silent. "I would like you to meet my beautiful granddaughter, Grace." One by one, she introduced her friends to Grace, who remembered to greet them all as "Auntie."

"Now let's eat," Lao Lao announced.

Grace got to see the Lazy Susan So, tell us, Grace, do you in action, as the different dishes revolved around the table for everyone to select. After practicing all week with Lao Lao, she used her chopsticks to eat everything. She could tell from her grandmother's smile that she was pleased.

After everyone was finished, Lao Lao rapped the table again. "Now we will talk about our book. Since Grace is our guest, we will speak only in English. Who would like to go first?"

"I will," said a take-charge woman with the dyed-blond hair. "Before we begin, I would like to let Grace know that I'm Evelyn Chen, David's grandmother. I understand you had dinner with him the other night."

Lao Lao interrupted, "They also spent the afternoon together today."

"I see," said Evelyn. "My grandson must be fond of you."

"Your grandson is such a good man," sweet-faced Auntie May said. "You must be very proud of him."

"I'm confused. Is he the one who's in medical school?" Auntie Connie asked in a raised voice.

"Yes, Connie," Auntie Jenny answered, patting her hands. "He's going into his third year, I believe. Isn't that right, Evelyn?"

Lao Lao spoke up again. "Why don't we let Grace answer Evelyn?"

Grace looked around at the five expectant faces. "David has been nice to me," she said with caution. "I appreciate his friendship."

"Tell us about yourself, Grace," Auntie Evelyn continued brusquely. "Are you also in school?"

"Yes, Auntie," she answered. "I'm going into my last year at NYU."

"Oh, NYU," Auntie Jenny said, clapping her hands. "That's a very good school, I hear."

"What are you studying?" Auntie Connie asked, her voice a decibel louder.

"I've taken mostly liberal arts courses," Grace explained. "I have taken a few premed classes, but I'm not sure that I want to continue in medicine."

"What will you do with your degree then, dear?" Auntie May chimed in sweetly.

"I . . . I'm not sure yet." Grace was starting to feel overwhelmed by all the questions.

"Why don't we let Grace decide for herself when the time comes," Auntie Evelyn said, declaring the matter closed.

Grace looked at her with relief.

"I believe this is a book group meeting," Lao Lao

interrupted again. "Why don't we discuss the book. Has everyone read *The Joy Luck Club*?"

"You know we have, Vivian," Auntie May said. "We all read it ages . . ." She put her hands over her mouth as if she had spilled the beans.

" . . .ages ago, and we're finally going to discuss it, aren't we?' Lao Lao finished Auntie May's words with a steely look, then turned to Grace. "Did you get a chance to read it? What did you think?"

"Well, I only read about half the book, but I think it's very good so far. It seems that growing up in China and growing up Chinese in America is very different. I guess you all experienced it with your own families."

"It's true," Auntie Evelyn said. "But I hear you've been reading some letters of a doctor who was in China during the late 1800s."

"Yes," Grace replied. "And I'd love to share it all with you."

"Some other time," Lao Lao said with emphasis. "We are discussing *The Joy Luck Club* tonight."

"Oh, come on, Vivian," Auntie Evelyn blurted out. "We read *The Joy Luck Club* years ago. Let's stop the deception and tell the girl the truth."

"I don't understand," Grace looked at Auntie Evelyn. What was she talking about?

Auntie Evelyn looked straight at her. "The truth is, we've been reading Dr. Hall's letters every month for a couple of years now. Each time we meet, we discuss another of his letters. For some unknown reason, your grandmother didn't want you to know."

Grace turned to her grandmother. "Lao Lao?"

12

No More Secrets

Silence, as everyone sat around the table, waiting for Grace's grandmother to speak. Just then, the doorbell rang. Grace went to answer the door. It was Mr. Albert Liu.

"What are you doing here?" Lao Lao stood when she saw him. "You know this is my night for the book club ladies."

"That's why I came tonight," Mr. Liu said. "I wanted to have the troops ready to help me." He gave her a gentle but firm push to the side and made his way down the hallway.

"What are you talking about?" Lao Lao said, following him. Her face was red, and she looked upset.

"I have made it possible for you to move to the Lotus Blossom Senior Community," he announced once he reached the dining room. "Sit down, Vivian, and I will explain."

As her grandmother sat with an annoyed grunt, Grace's head was spinning. She was so taken aback by this turn of events, she forgot the questions she had for Lao Lao. What was happening? What was Mr. Liu talking about?

Mr. Liu began. "I have been in contact with the senior community ever since we left earlier in the week. After some negotiations, I have obtained a two-bedroom apartment for you. You can keep your dining room table in the second bedroom. It's actually larger than this room."

Lao Lao sat upright. "It's not just my dining room table, it's also—"

"—it's the living room, too. I know," he said. "I've worked that out as well. You know how each floor has a large room for people to gather together? Management has agreed—in fact, they're delighted—to decorate that room on your floor with your living room furniture."

"That means people will be using it!" Lao Lao cried.

"That's right," Mr. Liu said. "And it's about time someone used it, don't you think?"

"That's a wonderful idea, Albert," said Auntie May with delight. "We could have dinner in Vivian's second bedroom, then discuss our reading in the meeting room. I've always wished I could sit in one of those beautiful Ming armchairs."

"There's more," Mr. Liu went on. "I plan to move into an apartment on the same floor of the Lotus Blossom Senior Community. I'm getting older myself and will enjoy the benefits."

"You!" Lao Lao sounded like she was accusing him.

He took her hand. "You may have turned down my proposals of marriage all these years, but you know you enjoy my company. Everyone here knows it. You will have your place, and I will have mine. So, whenever we tire of each other's company . . ."

The other book club ladies gave each other a knowing look.

Grace looked at Lao Lao, who was turning several shades of red.

"You think you can walk in here and tell me what to do? Just like that?" Lao Lao said, but her eyes were softening.

"Just like that," he said. "What do you say, Vivian? You get to keep all your furniture and maybe buy a few comfortable pieces for your own living room."

Auntie Jenny spoke up. "It's a beautiful place. I took a tour of it myself once. If you two are there, maybe I should move in."

"Me, too," Auntie May said with enthusiasm.

"Not right away," Mr. Liu said. "Give us enough time to have our honeymoon."

"Honeymoon, hah!" Lao Lao said before she paused. "I suppose it's okay . . . as long as I get to keep my furniture. But that's the only reason why I'm agreeing to it."

"Of course, Vivian," Mr. Liu said as he kissed her hand. "Of course."

Auntie Evelyn spoke up. "Congratulations, you two. But we still haven't answered the question about Mr. Hall's diaries."

"Ah, I see. Grace knows." Mr. Liu shook his head and looked at Lao Lao. "I warned you to tell her the truth, Vivian."

At this point, Grace didn't know whether to laugh or cry or be angry. It seemed that Lao Lao had kept quite a few secrets from her. And everyone knew about it but her. "Yes, Lao Lao," she said. "What exactly is the truth?"

Everyone in the room looked at Grace's grandmother.

"It's simple," she said, a bit on the defensive. "I wasn't sure how much Grace knew about her culture. My own daughter, Julie, has denied her background most of her life. I wanted Grace to be able to make her own decision about it."

"But why keep it a secret that you'd read Dr. Hall's letters yourself, Lao Lao?" Grace asked.

"I was afraid you wouldn't read them, Grace, unless I gave you a good reason," Lao Lao replied. "I had to coax you to do it when you first arrived."

"That's true," Grace admitted. "But why make up a story about a great grandmother working with him and trying to get the papers to his family?"

"Oh, that part is true!" Lao Lao said. "Dr. Hall's experiences need to be told to the world . . . and I thought . . . that maybe . . ."

Auntie Evelyn interrupted her. "For heaven's sake, Vivian, tell her." She turned to Grace. "She wants you to write a book about Dr. Hall and his experiences. We all do."

Grace was stunned. How did they know about her writing? Wait. She remembered what David had said. Her mother had been sending samples of her writing to Lao Lao for years. It suddenly dawned on her. Lao Lao, of course, shared them with Auntie Evelyn and the other book club ladies, and probably Mr. Liu. David knew because Auntie Evelyn had showed them to him. And Grace hadn't had a clue about any of it. Now everyone was looking at her for an answer.

"I'm flattered that you think I'm a good enough writer, but I've never written a book before. What makes you think I can do this? Also, what makes you think I *want* to do this?"

"You see, I warned you, Vivian," Auntie Evelyn said. "What if she doesn't *want* to write the book?"

"We all know she's capable," Lao Lao said. "So, tell us, Grace, do you *want* to write this book?"

With all the attention she was getting, Grace was beginning to feel as if she were in a cage at the zoo, and they were all waiting for her to perform a few tricks. "I'll have to think about it," she said at last. "I'm feeling a little overwhelmed right now." Grace excused herself and left the room.

A few minutes later, she was in her room, sitting in her Monk chair. As usual, she looked to Dr. Hall to feed her soul when her mind was jumbled. She'd been curious about the story of the leper. Dr. Hall called it "Life Is As a Bird of Passage." It didn't take her long to find it.

Wang Tien-pao was a leper. When first he came to the hospital begging relief, I was afraid to go near him. He dragged his weary body up the front steps and into the middle of the court. There, he tried to tell his story. The patients stood at a respectful distance away, but all were eager to hear him sing. Looking up at the faces of the interested folk, he began to sing:

"You honor me a foot and I'll honor you a rod.

You call me polished gentleman; I'll say you are a god!"

This was followed by . . .

"Eating food is a part of life for every day,

But eat not just to pass the time away!"

The first time I saw him, he was crawling along the street near the hospital, calling out his plea for food. His hands were gone to the wrists and his feet to the ankles. His face was swollen and all over his body were the tell-tale marks of the curse that held him in eternal bondage. Tied to his arm, he carried a wooden bowl. A string held it safe. As he crawled along the street, the bowl dragged on the stones. When food was offered, he gave a jerk to the bowl, and it always dropped right side up. When food was cast into the bowl, he lay down over it and ate the contents direct from it. He had no need for either a spoon or chopsticks.

The only home he had was a sort of pup tent on the bank of the river below the city. There he had many companions. It was their custom, when all were in for the night, to compare collections, and those who were most lucky divided their store with their less fortunate brothers. So far as I have ever been able to learn, this is the only communist community that is perfectly free from outside influence.

A local saying has it: "Sleep with a leper, but stay across the street from a man with the itch." I think that proverb lessens the dread of the disease with the people. He expressed great surprise that he was not ordered from the premises. He could not understand what manner of folk they were who would permit an outcast to breathe the same air with themselves. With due precaution, we gave him a careful examination and were compelled to tell him nothing could be done for his condition. Then he said he had heard someone read from a book that the great originator of this religion had cleansed many lepers and had also transferred that power to his followers. He had hoped the stories were true. Not that life meant so very much to him, but he thought it would be nice to go to his old home once again and look into the faces of his father and mother. Of course, they might not be in life now, but he must not complain. For seven years, he had been a wanderer, and no word had reached him about their condition. He said he had dreamed of sitting to tea with them without almost frightening them to death. His family lived in a great court with walls twenty feet high and thick in proportion. Before he became a victim of the curse, he had eaten the best food and swallowed the richest wine. His clothing was made of silk and linen, and he had long hair, always carefully groomed. No, he could not tell their name or where they live. Why, just think of it! Some one of the men standing before him might be his brother or a near relative, and he would not add sorrow to the life of any.

When he began to sing for me, I asked four of the patients to help me remember the words of his composition. When he had gone away, we compared notes, and the result was this.

LIFE IS AS A BIRD OF PASSAGE
 Life is as a bird of passage.
 Life begins, man knows not how;

Life goes, man knows not where;
Life ends, man knows not why!
Life is as a bird of passage.
For dishonesty it gives humiliation;
For bitterness it gives loathing;
For contention it give dismay;
For indifference it gives perplexity;
For despotism it gives censure;
For rudeness it gives retaliation;
For deception it gives chagrin;
For imposition it gives hazard;
For exaggeration it gives strife.
Life is as a bird of passage.
For cleverness it gives efficiency;
For caution it gives promotion;
For aspiration it gives ornament;
For benevolence it gives placidity;
For earnestness it gives veneration!
Life is as a Bird of Passage.'

Grace was struck by the leper's song and by his positive way of thinking. Although he'd been born wealthy and upper class, he accepted his horrible illness and didn't want to add sorrow to anyone else's life. He was willing to share any good fortune he had with his friends. And his song included such wisdom. Maybe it was time for her to jump on the bird of passage he called life. Maybe writing this book was part of that.

Grace heard a knock at the door. Mr. Liu poked his head in. "Are you alright?"

"I think so," Grace replied. "Thank you for convincing Lao Lao to make the move."

"You're welcome," he said. "They've all left now since the truth is out. I think they may have met their match in you."

"No, Uncle," she said. "I really did get caught up in Dr. Hall's writings. And Lao Lao is right. The world should get a chance to read what he experienced. I just don't know if I'm the one to tell his story."

Mr. Liu sat on the edge of her bed. "Remember, Grace, he's a good writer himself. You could include much of what he wrote in the book."

"But how do I organize it.?"

"Simple. Write about him the way you discovered him," Mr. Liu said. "How did you feel when you first read his letters and stories? What ideas did it generate in you?"

"You mean write about it, as if it's my story, too?"

"Isn't it?"

Grace paused for a moment to think back. She had come to Lao Lao's house against her will. She'd only started to read Dr. Hall's letters because her grandmother had pressured her. It wasn't long, though, before he'd started to grow on her. Every day, as she was learning more about China, she was learning more about herself. She'd come to admire Dr. Hall and the work he did. His people had become her people. Telling the story would be like opening up her true self to the world. Just this afternoon, she'd told David how important it was for people to read the letters and stories Hall had written.

"Uncle," she finally said.

"Yes, Grace."

"I think I *do* want to write Dr. Hall's story—as I experienced it."

He smiled, stood, and left her room.

A moment later, the phone rang. It was David. She was happy he called.

"Grace, are you okay?" he asked. "I drove my grandmother home from your house, and she told me what happened."

"I'm fine, David," she said. "Between Mr. Liu's announcement and my grandmother's secrets, it was too many surprises all at once. I think I've made up my mind, though."

"And?"

"And I've decided to try writing the book," she said.

"Great! I can't think of a better person to tell Dr. Hall's story," David said. "So . . . will you be sending all his material to your home in New Jersey? I guess you'll be able to work better there."

"Call me crazy, but I think I'll work on it here, over the summer. The book club ladies could give me their input on Dr. Hall's writing. I'm sure they'll have a lot to say. And Lao Lao still needs help moving all her furniture out. Plus, Mr. Liu is my Chinese history connection."

"I can't tell you how happy I am that you're staying," David said. "I'll give you as much help as I can. It'll . . . you know . . . give us more time to get to know each other."

"Yeah," Grace said. "I thought of that, too."

"Tomorrow's Sunday," he said, "so I'm still free. Want to go for a ride somewhere?"

"Sure, why not?" Grace answered. "Wait. That didn't come out right." What better time to speak the truth, she thought. "I'd love to spend the afternoon with you, David Chen." There. She'd said it.

Having opened a new door, she decided it was time to close an old one. She called Adam back. Her message to him required more than a text.

"What is it now?" Adam answered. She could still hear talking and laughter in the background.

Grace took a deep breath. "Just wanted you to know that we're over. I don't need a boyfriend who's cold, offensive, and doesn't care enough about me to listen when I need to talk to him."

"Wait, babe, what are you . . .?"

"I'm dumping you, Adam," she said with confidence.

"But Gracie, babe," he whined.

"I'm not your Gracie, babe, anymore, Adam," she added with a new sense of power. "Oh, and by the way, Adam . . . what I wanted to tell you? I'm Chinese. Got that? And I'm proud of it. I don't care if you like it or not!"

"You're Chi—"

Grace hung up before he had a chance to say anything.

After the call to Adam, Grace found Lao Lao in the kitchen, washing dishes. She kept her back to Grace.

"I guess you're leaving," Lao Lao said, "just like your mother."

"Lao Lao, look at me." said Grace.

Lao Lao turned around and Grace took her hands. "I'm not leaving, Lao Lao. I'm staying all summer. I'm going to help you and Mr. Liu move into the Lotus Blossom Senior Community. And I'm going to write a book about Dr. Hall, at least about his first few years in China, so I hope you're not in too much of a hurry to sell this place."

Lao Lao grasped both of Grace's hands. "Oh, Grace. I know you will make a wonderful book. You are such a good writer."

"I'll also have a conversation with my mother about sending you those pictures of me and everything I've written, apparently, since kindergarten." Grace folded her arms. She was deciding the best way to put what she intended to say next. "You and Mom, Lao Lao. This has to end. You're missing out on each other's lives. I hope you and I can work on a way to get through to her this summer."

Lao Lao nodded. "I'll do my best."

"Good," Grace said. "And if I'm going to be an official Chinese American, you'll have to teach me how to cook some of your Chinese recipes."

Lao Lao laughed. "Nothing would make me happier."

"And thank you, Lao Lao, for encouraging me to read Dr. Hall's letters," she said. "I've learned a lot about my culture, and I'm sure there'll be more lessons to come. At first, I thought I wasn't like any of the people Dr. Hall wrote about. But I understand them better now. They had two thousand years of philosophy and religious belief that shaped their habits, superstitions, and ideas—the importance of rituals, family honor and respect, and reliance on natural elements such as herbs for healing. It's true that they often lost track of common sense. But aren't we all guilty of that? Was the addiction to opium in China any different from the drug addiction in our society today? And wasn't it q misunderstanding that drove you and my mother apart?"

Lao Lao's eyes were filled with tears. "I'm so sorry, Grace."

She held Lao Lao's hands. "I want to be like Dr. Hall. I want to share his words so that everyone can learn how foolish we all can be at times. I want the world to know what he knew—that we all deserve to be treated with love and respect, no matter what mistakes we make."

"And one last thing," she said to her grandmother. "No more secrets!"

Lao Lao put her hand on her heart. "I promise."

Back in her room, Grace picked up her notebook from the top of the dresser, sat down in the Monk chair, grabbed a pen from the table, took a deep breath, and began to write.

DR. HALL'S JOURNAL

The original journal from Doctor Hall

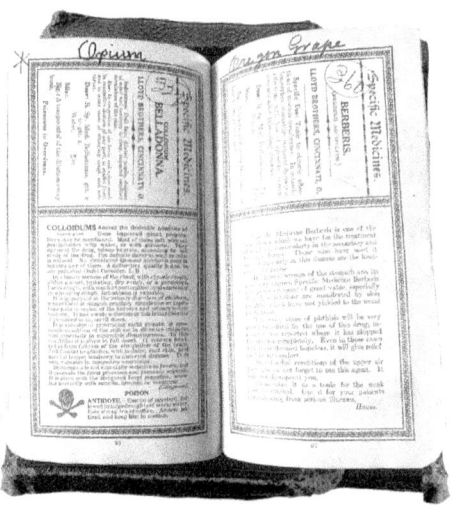

Herbs for Opium Treatment

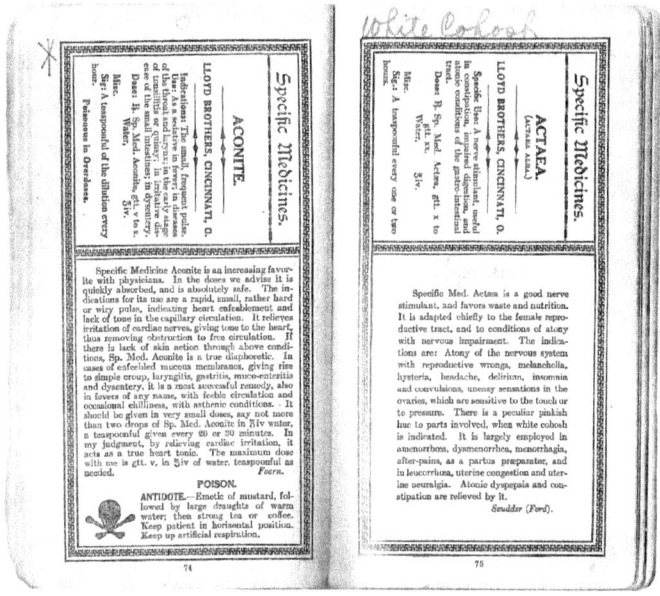

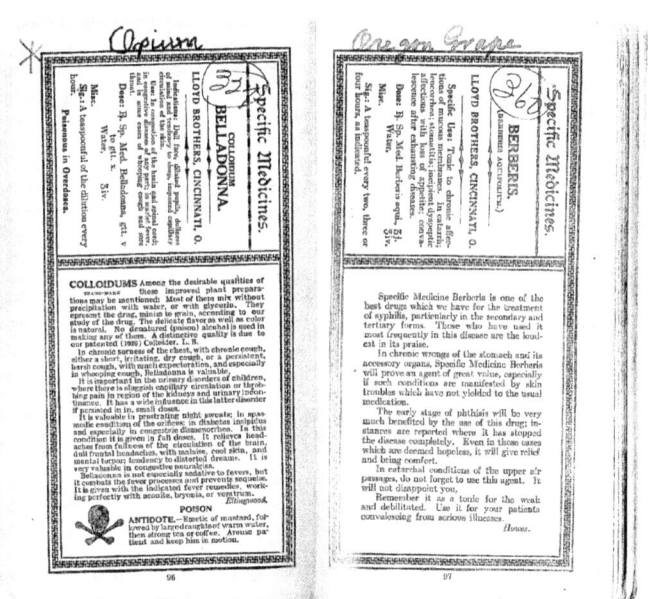

Herbs for Opium Treatment

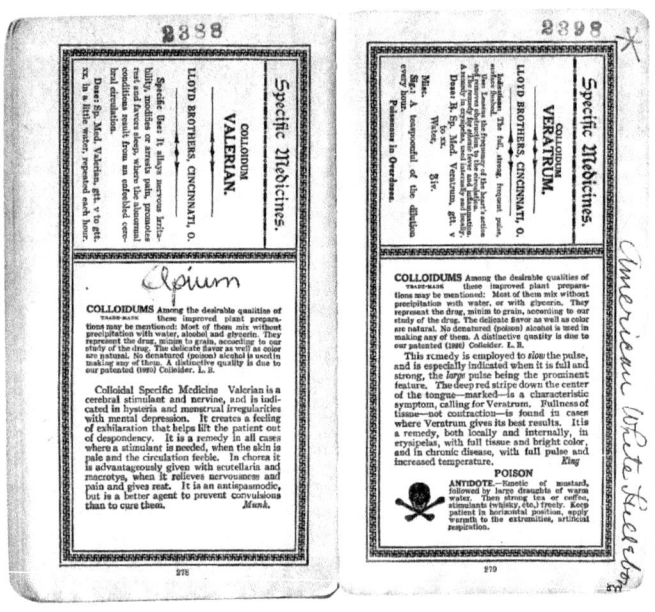

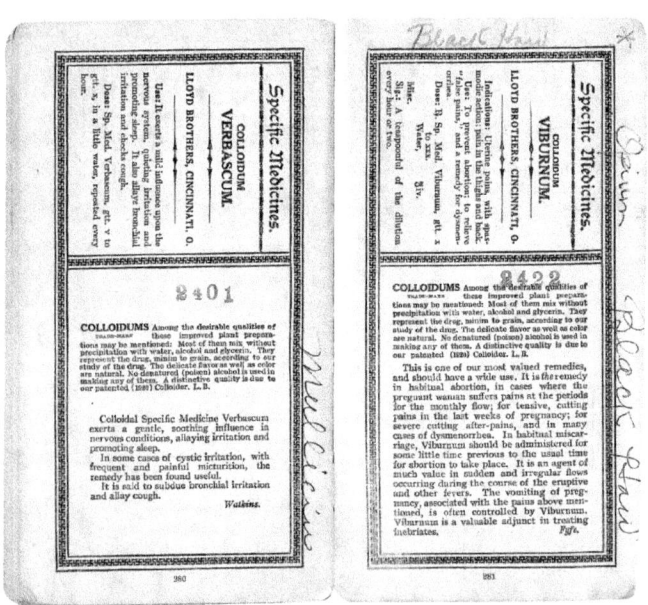

Herbs for Opium Treatment

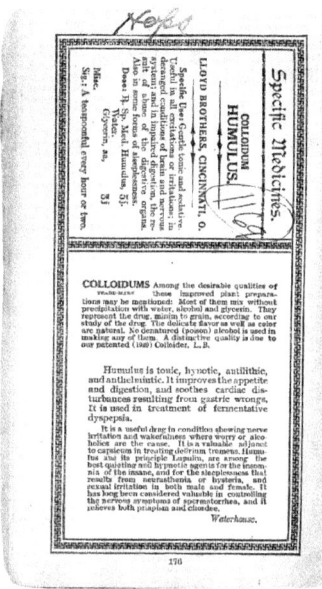
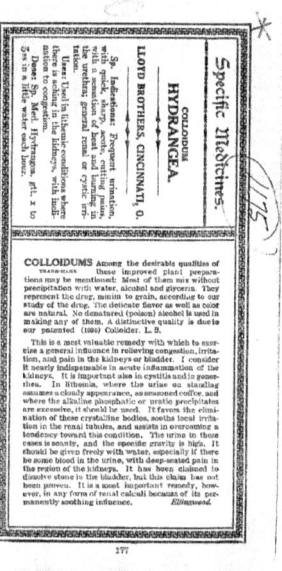

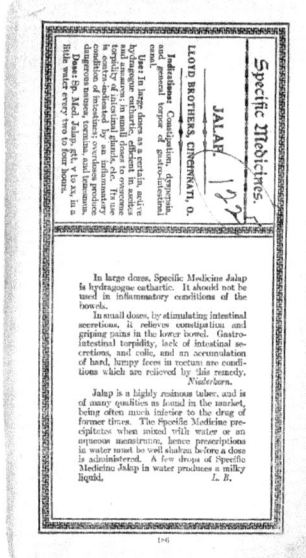
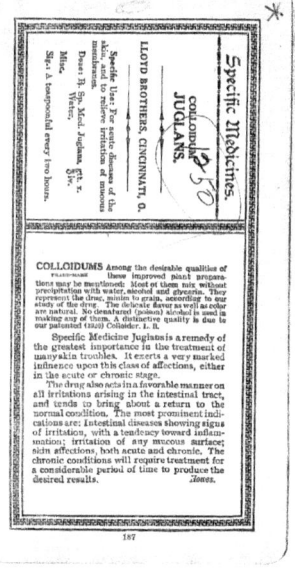

Chapter 3 - The Fox and the Kitchen God

Letter No. 3.

Liman, Shansi, China,
October, 1896.

The fox sometimes bewitches a man.
I have seen one man, in this village,
who is both respected and feared by
reason of this possession. That he is
a privileged character is proven by
the fact that he does not wear his
hair long – as is the common rule.
The fox also has the power of transformation, or whatever you please to
call it. On certain nights during
this moon this animal is said to
appear as a most beautiful woman. The change is wrought
in an instant. Fire in two long
flames issues from its mouth, the
eyes flash and grow bright until
the sight of the spectator is overpow-
er by the radiance thereof. Then the
change comes. Only for a few minutes, just after midnight, may this
be witnessed. And fortunate the
man who sees the change. I asked a number of men if this was
a fact and was answered always

The Fox and the Kitchen God

in the affirmative. "Have you ever
witnessed the change?" "No! I have
not, but I have heard of men who
had been fortunate." Thus it goes,
the people do not try to investigate such a thing. Superstition,
associated as it is with ignorance
and an utter lack of the spirit of
investigation, forms a barrier to
our Christian teaching. The fox
has, also, during this moon, the power of healing all diseases. The
great obstacle in the way of all
the people taking advantage of
his wondrous skill is the diffi-
culties experienced in meeting him.
But the people believe he can heal
disease, for men have been heard
to say that until they were treated
by the fox their complaints were
many — now the body has no
illness at all. When a man
is bewitched he acquires a peculiar power. He can treat Diphtheria! Lucky the village
which has a fox-man, should

The Fox and the Kitchen God

it be visited by this dread disease.
He alone can fight the evil demon-
dragon which brings Diphtheria.
A few years since this village
was cursed by the dragon and the
Diphtheria came. Liman had no
fox-man to treat or prevent
the ravages of the scourge. Men
and women, as well as the children fell before it. As a last
resort, application was made to
the magistrate for relief. He
issued this order, — "Any compound
which has had ten cases of Diphtheria may claim to have a
fox-man." Less than
three hundred yards from our
gate, by the great gate of an extensive compound I saw a small
block of wood nailed to the wall.
On this is written two characters —
giving notice to the demon=dragon
that the compound had a fox-
man. The dragon, on seeing these
characters, dares not enter. I asked the number of cases of Diphtheria

The Fox and the Kitchen God

20

"Was there more than ten?" "Oh, no, only one little girl, not the chief man of the compound, fearing his own son might die, purchased from the magistrate the right to use the warning sign."

A few days since, while I was attempting to explain to a patient the functions of the brain and its relations to the different portions of the body, I secured an idea of the belief of the people of this place on the subject. On saying to him that reason and government and emotion and passion were supposed to originate in the brain, he replied, "No, doctor, you are all wrong. The seat of reason and love and passion is not in the head, but in the stomach! There are only two exceptions to this rule. The cock reasons from its comb. The first faint rays of light strike its comb and it immediately announces the approach of day! The wolf's

The Fox and the Kitchen God

reasons is neither in its head nor in its body, but in its legs. When the wolf sees an image of the dragon, its legs immediately drag its body around and make off with it.'" The lesson was postponed to some future, indifinite time!

These two stories will, I trust, give you some idea of the obstacles we meet in our work. In themselves the stories may be interesting or amusing, but to us, here on the field, knowing and feeling that such ideas and influences prevail, they bring a feeling of sadness which words cannot express. The masses of the people may be simple-minded. I suppose they are, but just such beliefs as these must be overthrown ere we can claim any particular person for God. The people are such a strange mixture of superstition and contradiction. Altho' for the most part you would

think their gods infallible from
their point of view, yet we are
daily proofs, by the people giv-
en, that even the wisest of
their gods are extremely gullible. To illustrate. The Kitch-
en god, of which I have spoken,
is very fond of a certain kind
of candy. The people, knowing
his weakness for this particular
sweet-meat, take advantage of
his god-ship in a most unkind way. It would never
do for this god to go up to heaven
and tell of all their sins of omission and commission. The god's
throat is small. The people prepare this particular candy in
round hollow balls, small
enough to go into his mouth,
but too large to enter the throat.
These balls are placed with the
other offerings. The god on seeing his favorite immediately
fills his mouth. It will not
go down and he will not give

The Fox and the Kitchen God

it up, so away to heaven he must go, with his mouth so full it is not possible to say a word. Poor old god! And yet, these people think of this same kitchen god as their patron saint. They fall down before his image and make obeisance as tho' their lives and their happiness depended on his gracious pleasure.

Our religion does not bid us bow to gods of stocks and stone. Our Blessed Master tells us that He is the Way, the Truth and the Life, and that to be saved all must come to him. Oh the peace He gives to us, when we try to serve him! How true are the words

"I know not where His islands lift Their fronded palms in air, I only know we cannot drift Beyond His love and care."

May this people be brought into a knowledge of His love and care!

Very Truly, Yours W. L. Hall.

Chapter 4 & 5 -
Cleanliness, Bones, and the Chinese Doctor

Letter No. 6,

Liman, Shansi, China.
January, 1897,

Dear friends:—

As I review the past years work a longing comes o'er me - I want to tell you something about it. I feel sure you will all be interested in hearing of our work in the hospital - for us with these people. This has been, as you know, my first full years work in China. Not much was accomplished during 1895 - we were only preparing for good things to come. I have kept a (somewhat) accurate clinic report - this report I will be pleased to send to as many of you as may desire a copy, when it is issued.

During the year I saw and treated one thousand, eight hundred and sixty eight cases. (1868). These patients come from far and near, — if one patient comes from a village we expect more. Diseases, which to these people seem

Cleanliness, Bones, and the Chinese Doctor

beyond remedy are often entirely cured
and all evidences thereof removed,
with cleanliness and by the application of simple remedies. One
of our first duties appears to be
to impress on the minds of the
patients that cleanliness is essential to recovery. For instance,
a patient comes to me with a wound
on the hand, caused by running
a chisel into the flesh. To look
at the man, with his whole arm
wrapped and bundled, it would seem
that he feared a death-wound.
I first remove the garment wrapped around the outside — then
I find the long sleeves (all of them)
brought down over the hand and
a string tied around the ends. After many protests — "fear cold", fear
cold" — from patient and many assurances by me, "no fear, no fear" —
he unties the string, slowly loosens
out the folds; glances around the
room to see if it has any openings for "cold" to enter, asks if

Cleanliness, Bones, and the Chinese Doctor

the door is securely fastened, if I
expect to run a needle thro'
his hand (the Chinese way of treating all diseases – i.e, run a
long iron or silver needle into
the seat of disease, to kill the
evil spirit who has taken up its
abode in that part), or will I
give medicine to rub on or to
take internally, etc, etc,
Finally, on my assuring him that
I must first see his hand and
that he must leave the room for
other patients who are waiting, if
he does not want me to treat
him, the sleeves are pulled up
to the elbows and we find, – not
the hand, but a little cloth bag –
tied around the wrist and just
large enough for the hand to go
in, – After we convince the man
that all must be removed, he takes
his hand out of the bag, removes
the cloths that are wound and
wound around it, and at last
holds up his hand for in-

Cleanliness, Bones, and the Chinese Doctor

spection. As yet I can see nothing
except a mass of black. The
hand was covered with black
dirt, or coal dust, when he received the wound, and had not been
disturbed. I cannot describe to
you, on paper, (I'll tell you when I
see you) the expressions of that face
and the ohs! and ahs! when the assistant turns a stream of warm
water on to the hand. Do we dare
use water? After the hand is
clean I find the wound. It was
small at first, but pus formed
and unable to escape, had burrowed in among the tendons and a-
round the bones. "How many days?"
I ask. "Eighteen". No wonder it
is in bad condition! We use a
simple dressing, bind it up
lightly and the man goes away
happy. A few dressings usually
restore the hand to its natural
condition, unless the man takes
opium. Opium users are more
difficult to treat, for any complaint.

I give you this instance not as an exception but as a type of what we see. Let the wound be what it will, let the disease be located in any part of the body, it is a task for the patient to risk his life by exposing himself to "cold". The day may be sultry, but that mysterious something, designated "cold", is ever present. One of the fixed ideas with this people seems to be a desire to have all the bones of the body buried together. They do not readily agree to the removal of a bone, or part of one. Some most amusing cases are seen — especially in cases where it is best to remove an aching tooth. I have had persons come for relief whose teeth would be so loose that they would turn this way and that, and when closed together they would turn in and out. The owners would come because, as they said "when I eat my teeth do

Cleanliness, Bones, and the Chinese Doctor

not eat." But they often refuse to part with their teeth. They ask me if I have a plan, whereby I can push the tooth back into its place and make it eat! (Have heard of artificial teeth, possibly). One old man, whose two remaining teeth I would not guarantee to make "eat," went away lovingly turning them this way and that, with his tongue, and assured me "I want not to separate my bones." One woman, whose tooth dropped out when I took hold of it with my fingers, flew into a great passion, cried and spat at her serving woman by turns and pounded the floor with her stick. (I think she wanted to pound the doctor). On inquiry I learned that she had come to have the tooth fastened not removed.

Many such interesting cases are met, – some arousing mirth, but the great majority awaking pity. The people are grateful for services rendered, I know, and some of

Cleanliness, Bones, and the Chinese Doctor

Their simple demonstrations go right to
our hearts. And, then, we find it so
easy to tell them of a place where
disease and pain and separation
are unknown. That they have a
Friend and Saviour who is also their
Friend and Saviour. It is our endeav-
or to impress on each patient
the fact that the gospel, with its
love and pity and its redemption
is of greater importance than any
earthly joy or sorrow. That when
we are in possession of the gift
of God, — the redemption through
Jesus Christ, His son, — our earthly
ills sink into insignificance when
compared with the joys of that home
in Heaven. If we are His, it
matters not to us, where our bodies
lie, or what part goes first, — we
are His and He will care for us.
Oh, the blessed reward we have, even
while in this life, when we see the
look of peace on the faces of our
people here, when they begin to understand and long for and accept.

Cleanliness, Bones, and the Chinese Doctor

It is not for us to know the result of the years work. We do know that the future holds much in store for this Empire. The time is coming when China will be called Christian — our faith is strong in the promises.

I closed the hospital on the 15th of this month, for Chinese New Year. Will open again on 20th February. I have had the regular clinics for out-patients and have seen nearly two hundred patients for the month, coming from more than 20 villages.

Speaking of the Chinese doctors using the needle reminds me of an instance I saw last year at the fair, in a large market town near Simao. Two doctors(?) had a tent on one of the main streets. In this tent they treated any and all diseases. I saw them operate on a man for some eye disease. I could not get close enough to ascer-

Cleanliness, Bones, and the Chinese Doctor

tain the nature of the complaint. One of the doctors examined the eye, said a few words of some unknown "gibberish," made a few passes before the mans face and announced that the man was "ready to be healed." He then pinched up, the skin on the mans forehead, above the nose, and taking a needle about six inches long, thrust it into the skin, bringing it out about two inches from point of entrance. Next, taking up the cheek, he thrust a needle through it, the point entering about one-fourth inch from angle of the mouth, passing thro' cheek into mouth; point was then carried backward toward angle of jaw and brought out thro' the flesh as near the ear as possible — the point was elevated somewhat, and passed up over the top of the ear, on the outside — the other cheek was then "treated" in the same manner.

Cleanliness, Bones, and the Chinese Doctor

He then used a piece of iron as
follows:- viz.- Placing one end of
the iron firmly against the man's
temple; the other end held in the
palm of his hand and the back
of his hand up against his
left shoulder, with his right
hand he drew what seemed a
small iron rod with links attached, rapidly back and forth
across the rod and at right angles with it. This rasping noisy
performance was continued for
perhaps half a minute, when
letting go the iron rod, chain and
all, he sprang to a small table
standing me near, grasped something between his thumb and
forefinger, sprang back to his
patient and thrust a small short
needle, with a head like an upholstery tack, but much larger,
into the spot where had rested the
end of the iron rod. The twinge
as the needle struck the skull
was most unpleasant. The

other temple received the same treatment. There were now "one needle thro' the forehead, & one thro' each cheek, & one in each temple. Now an incense stick, about three inches long, lighted at one end was laid over (resting) on top of each ear. Some substance was then lighted and stuck on the points of the needles over the ear. These slowly burned away the patient meanwhile sitting immovable, unmoved by any part of the barbaric proceeding. When the cotton (or whatever it was) had burned, leaving the needle hot, the needles were drawn out with a jerk — then those in the temples were withdrawn and last of all that from the forehead. The man was pronounced "well", the doctor told him to "go" and turning to another patient said "This man is ready to be healed."

Comment unnecessary.

Yours, Very Truly,
W L Hall.

Chapter 6 - The Crowded Hospital

Letter No. 7

Liman, Shansi, China.
Feby 1897.

This letter must be short. I do not find time these days to write to any of my friends as I would wish.

I went to Tai Yüen Fu, the capital of the Province, on the 16th of this month. There we had a Conference, of missionaries and native Christians. It was a season of refreshing, from the first service, at 7 pm. Saturday, to the Communion service at 7 pm. Tuesday. The services were all in Chinese. More than two hundred persons were present at some of the meetings. Questions of vital importance were discussed, by the natives, from a native standpoint, and by the missionaries. The bodies participating were (1) English Baptist Mission, (2) American Board Mission, (3) British and Foreign Bible Society, (4) Shes Yang Mission (5) China Inland Mission, (6) Tai Yüen Fu Mission

An organization to be known as "The Central Shansi Christian Conference" was effected and it was decided to meet annually, in Tai Yüen Fu. The native Christians were happy, and I am sure all were greatly benefitted. They were brought together from different parts of the field, and I feel sure each will return to his home a more earnest worker for God. Ninety-seven (97) natives were at Communion on Tuesday evening.

When I opened the hospital on the 20th Chinese, (Feby 21st), as that was Sunday I received only two inpatients. On Monday they came in great numbers. I had to say "no hope" to many, and these returned to their homes. When I felt that I could help any one I told them to stay. I now have more than seventy (70) inpatients — more than fifty (50) are in the opium refuge. Come with me for one day's work and I am sure you will excuse my short letter. I see each of these patients three times a day — morning, noon, and night. I also go to their rooms at other times during the day and night, to see if they are comfortable. I also see the men at morning prayers (10 o'clock) and when I can find time I go to afternoon prayers (3 p.m.). I am also called up at night to see patients who are suffering — suffering untold agony in the effort to leave off the terrible drug. The patients have begged to come offering to sleep anywhere if I would only give my permission. They are sleeping on the native beds and on the floor, on piles of straw. Fourteen are now sleeping in the chapel on doors and benches. They are anxious to leave off the opium so they can plant their crops. I have turned away more than fifty persons from the opium refuge as I could not put them anywhere. They have offered to sleep in the cellar — but this

The Crowded Hospital

57

I could not allow. Some of these opium patients are also under treatment for other diseases. My clinics are full — on the 24th of Feb, between 80 and 90 people were in the court. During the day eleven carts came, bringing patients. I am very busy, but I am not complaining. We need more help — especially do we pray for a young lady to work with the women. They have no one to visit them regularly and so much peace and happiness will come to any one who will come. Who will it be? Are not some of you ready to come?

I will try to write more in March.

Our lady, Lois has been very ill. Day and night have we watched her, and the dear Lord has given her to us for a comfort. We are thankful to him for for His mercy.

"God be with you all."

Yours, "In His name"

W L Hall

Chapter 6 - The Opium Curse

"I want my mother! I want my mother." –
The dirty little waif, standing by the roadside looked the picture of despair. The
wind was blowing, oh, so cold and the little five year old could, with difficulty, re-
tain its footing. Its outer garment was
unbuttoned and the tapes – mute witness
of sex – were loose on its feet. We were
near a village. A man came hurriedly round a corner. He was evidently
a servant in search of something. His
attention was drawn to the foreigner and
some time passed before he saw the
tiny object of his search. He sprang to (at)
the child, grasped it by the arm and with
an oath, started at a rapid pace toward
the village. As he passed our cart I said,
"your child?" "No! I have no need for such
a little pest!" "It wants its mother. Is
she living?" "Yes, it does, but it will
not get her." I started my "pump"
and succeeded in getting part, at least,
of the child's history. As I cannot give
my questions and his answers as they
come I must tell you the story as I
translated it.

The Opium Curse

"Sad, sad. This child's father is a member of one of the wealthy families of our village. He has taken opium for more than ten years and all his money is gone. His servants robbed him and his neighbors cheated him. He married ten years ago. His wife was one of the most beautiful girls. She has never taken opium and has always worked hard to keep her children and herself in clothing and food. Just before the last New Year the man had no money and he must have opium. He told his wife, one day to dress the two children – he wanted to go on the street. Two children – this girl and a boy three years old. The mother followed them to the door, and stood looking after them. Some time after she went to her husband's room. He was lying on the kang, smoking opium. She asked for the children. He said do not fear they will return. They did not return and the mother was almost dead. She went on the street asking for the children. She traced them to my

The Opium Curse

master's home. She rushed into the
court and on into the room. Her
girl – this girl – was sitting on the
floor, crying. She picked it up, started out the door and had almost
reached the front gate when my master came out of his room, struck
her, said "this is my child. I bought
it from your husband today for five
thousand cash" – and pushed her out.
He closed the door and the mother
started to her home, wailing as she
went. Some one who knew the circumstances said "your husband
sold your little boy to a man from
Yang tsun and the man took him
away in his cart. He got seven ounces
of silver for the boy." The woman
went home, crying as loud as she could.
She tried to talk with her husband but
he was sleeping – the opium was doing
its work. The money was gone in a
few days. The New Year was soon to come
all at once the man had plenty of
opium. He would not tell his wife
where he got it. The day before the

The Opium Curse

New Year he told his wife to put on her nicest clothing and they would go see the children. She hurried and they were soon in the cart. They entered the court of one of the richest men. The woman said they were in the wrong court and told the carter to return. But they went into the court and on into the rooms occupied by the rich man's wives. The woman went in and sat on the kang, while the rich man and her husband went on to another room. Soon the rich man came in and the woman asked for her husband. "He has gone home. I bought you from him for ten ounces of opium and thirty thousand cash. You are mine, not his." The woman cried, but that was all she could do"
—— The man went on, our carter called to his mule, and we passed on thro the village. Sad, sad indeed! And The story is told in a few sentences but the sorrow and shadow over the life of that loving mother-heart can not be expressed in words. And

The Opium Curse

our hearts are saddened when we know that such cases are constantly seen here. It is not uncommon for a man to sell wife and children and home and all for the cursed drug. Having seen some of the actors in this life-tragedy I am more interested in it.

This Province has been the boast of China. But the end is coming. The area planted to opium increases year by year — the users of the vile destroyer are rapidly increasing in number. As opium comes in peace and plenty and prosperity go out. Opium is, at this time, the greatest obstacle to the advance of the Cross. Opium makes its votaries forget sin and blunts the perception into a semi-imbecile indifference to all influences for good.

May the Lord send help.

Yours, Very Truly,

A. L. Hall.

Chapter 7 - Only a Girl

Letter No 8.

Liman, Shansi, China
March 1897.

"Not important! not important! its only a girl! its only a girl." The speaker seemed in earnest. He would have me understand what it was he said. The man had come to me for medicine for his child. I had just said to him that I could treat the child better if he would bring her to the hospital. "But my home is far away", he said. "How far?" "Thirty li" (10 miles). I then said if you consider your child important you will surely bring it." "Not important! not important! its only a girl! its only a girl." — Poor little girl she was not important. Had she been a boy nothing would have been too good for him. but she was "only a girl". The boys in China are considered Heaven's choicest blessings — the girls are only marks & evidences of Heaven's displeasure. But I am not to tell you of China as a nation, I want to tell you of China's little children, as I see them!

Only a Girl

My story will not be pleasant. I can see so little in the lives of these dear little ones that could be called happiness or even comfort. When a girl baby comes to a home no demonstration is made — the father is considered unfortunate, the mother unlucky. Poor little waif! Not a word of welcome, not a loving caress — except by the poor mother. Mother-love seems to exist the world over. If the family is large or if the older children are girls the little visitor does not remain long. The nurse either strangles it at once, or it is cast aside to die. Wrapped in a bundle of hay it is carried on to the wall if in a city, and dropped over. — if in a village it is carried outside the village. This is done at night. You will ask "what becomes of the bodies". Ah, the wolves and the dogs make short work of all that is given them. The bundle is quickly torn open and the little one is no more! These little piles of straw are every where visible

But each pile does not represent a murder. They have a further use, as I will show later. And I would not have you think every family despises little girls — I only tell you some of the things which exist in a country that is not christian. But we will presume that we are in a family that does not want to murder its little daughter. The little one is preserved and is expected to grow up into a young lady. Soon we see a plump happy baby — they walk and talk early — and after a fashion can play around the room or in the court. For three years all may go well — then comes to the little life something over which it has no control — the mother does not let it go barefoot. (I have not seen ten barefooted children since I came to China that I remember). If it could only wear its shoes well and good, But it cannot. — or, it is not allowed to do so. With strong cotton tape the little feet are bound — beginning at the toes, the tape is wound around

Only a Girl

up to the ankle. These tapes are gradually tightened. The little body increases in size - the little feet cannot. By the tenth year the feet are usually out of shape - the toes are doubled and pressed together, the heel is elevated by means of small round blocks of wood, the weight of the body is on the toes and the ball of the foot - and a life of misery is the result. The bones of the foot are crushed, bent or broken. The smaller the foot the more fashionable!

I have seen little girls five or six years old, sitting on the ground or on the doorsteps who would be continually putting the hands to the feet — they would cry and sometimes try to loosen the bandages but to no avail. The little hands would stroke the aching, throbbing feet, while the eyes, mute witnesses of the unspeakable agony — would fill with tears. The faces often assume an habitual expression of suffering. How sad it all appears to us! Now the little

Only a Girl

one cannot run and play. She can only hobble around — she must rest every few minutes — she must not complain she dare not alter her condition. When she attains the age of twelve or thirteen years she is sold to some family as a wife for their son. Sometimes these little girls are taken to the homes of their intended husbands and supported by the family. This is not the usual method, but I have known of it in a few cases. And our little friend cannot be called free even yet. She has now become the personal property of her husband's mother — and that mother can make her miserable if she chooses to do so. So long as this mother lives the daughter-in-law must serve her — but she is a woman now, and as such we shall not further discuss her for a letter devoted to children. The girl who goes to school or is taught lessons in language is the _rare_ exception.

Only a Girl

How different when a son is born!
A son is important! He must be
cared for and his slightest wish
is law. He must be protected
from disease and from the myriad evil spirits which exist.
Some friend of the family (or some
relative will do) "locks him to life".
This ceremonial I do not know—
but I have seen some very dirty
strings and bands and metal
strips around the necks of some
of my little patients. I am told
that the article is fastened on to
remain until the child's twelfth
birthday! The condition of the
amulet is not important—the intention is all important. Nothing
would induce a parent to remove
the charm for an instant. Holes
are made in little girl's ears soon
after birth — girls, babies, women and
grandmothers wear ear rings. Girls
are "not important". The spirits do not
trouble girls. — they want boys! I have
seen baby boys with a ring in one

Chapter 7 - Bad Mother-in-Law

Letter No. 16. 45

Liman, Shansi, China.
November, 1897

Would you have a few notes from my case=book? Well, I will give them to you.

Case No. — received into hospital last of August. Female, age 19, with a baby two years old. The husband brought his wife for treatment and visited her a number of times during her stay in the hospital. The woman was suffering from a disease which yielded readily to treatment. She was taken away by her husband in September — was in the hospital about a month. She was bright and quick to learn; anxious to be taught and seemed interested in the Gospel. She manifested great affection for her little one and when her husband came they seemed a happy family. Today, (Nov. 20th) I was called to the woman's court to see a patient, — the boy said

Bad Mother-in-Law

one of our old patients had returned.
The woman was carried from the cart
to her room by her father and the carter. Between moans the poor girl
told her story — which was assert-
ed to by her father and mother.
She had returned to her home happy
in her restoration to health.
She could help with the work and
divide the cares of the humble
household. She was well and so
all looked bright. But she had
incurred the enmity and displeasure of her husband's mother —
her owner. The mother-in-law
said she was well now and she
would be always running about.
She was better sick, for then she
could not leave the room. The
task-master began to prove her power.
Her tongue was harder to bear than
her tasks. At length she began on the
husband. Why had he taken his wife
away from home for a month! Why
had he proven so ungrateful to his
old mother! A pretty son, he was.

Bad Mother-in-Law

The best thing he could do was to beat
his wife — that would make her
good!" And just see this baby. Its mother has been sitting
around talking no eating no
has neglected the child. Beat
her, beat her! You won't beat her!
You dare speak thus to your mother! Undutiful son! Then
she went into a (convenient) fit
and announced that she would
put an end to all this trouble
and to her life at the same time.
They then began pleading with her,
but to no avail. There was only one
way to avert her death — if the son
would beat his wife with her
(the mother's) stick, she would be
his mother still, Otherwise —
The man, to save his mother's
life took up the stick and began
beating his wife. He beat her over
the head and shoulders until she
fell over on her face, then on the
back and limbs until his mother
came out of her "fit" and told

Bad Mother-in-Law

him she was satisfied. The girl was unable to rise, and she plead to come to him and to the doctor. The mother would not let her come — she kept her in sight to the better vent her spleen. The husband had to go to his work — a shop in a distant town. When he should go the mother would have to nurse the girl. That she did not choose to do, so ordered the husband to load his wife into a cart and take her to her mother. The girls parents brought her soon as possible. Her body is beaten black and blue — the tears come and you can see her hands clench from the pain when she moves. I have made the poor aching body as comfortable as I can and will do all that is possible to remove from her body all evidence of this, one of China's darkest, most hopeless customs — the tyranical rule of the mother-in-law.

Bad Mother-in-Law

The threat to take life is common, but not always in earnest. Not long ago a woman on the place told her thirteen-year-old daughter to do some piece of work. The girl refused and a war of words resulted. As the mother's climax she said she would kill the girl — the girl that she would kill herself! The girl started for a well in the garden adjoining the woman's court. The mother picked up a stool and started after her. The girl was four or five paces in advance — neither could run — neither could walk fast — not a word was spoken. Waddling along on their crippled feet on such awful errand party I confess I was tickled rather than frightened. Four or five persons ran after the couple — some pleading with the mother to spare her daughter, others begging the girl to spare herself. I passed thro the court in a short time. The pleadings had prevailed — the mother would

Bad Mother-in-Law

spare her daughter for this once.
The begging was not so successful,
the girl sat on the ground near the
well and threatened to throw herself
in if any one dare approach her.
I dated. I thought the farce had gone
far enough, I asked if the girl really would kill herself? "Sure, if you
go near." I went up to the girl
and asked her, as a special favor
to me, to jump into the well at
once if she intended doing so—
and would she please tell me if
the water was cold. The people saw
that the girl failed to disappear
down the well, they began to laugh,
she began to cry and I moved on.
A little later mother and daughter were
smacking their lips over the same
dish of food and all was well.

Many poor women do put an
end to their troubles and they
are not all mothers-in-law.
Young women die to escape the
mother-in-law – the mean ones.
Many are kind and gentle and lovable.

Bad Mother-in-Law

Thanksgiving. — The members of the station are together today. Our blessings are beyond telling — we are all happy in the Master's service.

One of the patients sent in word early this morning that he must return to his home at once. He was in the opium refuge who had been here only one third of the regular time. We all tried to keep him, but the exhortations and pleadings were in vain. He had dreamed a dream. He saw some member of his family. He must go. It was a warning. He could not sleep. Arose at two or three o'clock and walked the courts until day. The people fear dreams. They are in constant dread if they dream of any of their people. The spirit of some departed ancestor is calling for company. The man went away in seeming agony.

Two little boys, nine or ten years

Bad Mother-in-Law

old, came standing at the front gate, when I went out this forenoon. They were in rags. One had a small basket and each carried a little bag. The thermometer stood at about 29°+ the wind was blowing. I asked what were they doing. "Looking ashes for bits of coal". I told them to come in and took them to a pile of ashes from the stove in the chapel. They could not believe me when I said they might pick the ashes. But I convinced them at last and then those cold dirty fingers fairly flew in and out and thro that pile of ashes. The bodies shivered and the rags danced in the wind, and as I stood near, talking to them their little tongues were loosened and told me many things of the emptiness and desolateness of their lives. Time after time they went thro the ashes and when they were ready to go all that remained was barely enough to mark the spot.

(To be continued). Yours very truly,
W. S. Hall

Chapter 7 - A Slave No Longer

Liman, Shansi, China
January 1898.

A patient returned to her home on the 2nd. of December. She was in the opium refuge. A man came in today (Jan. 18) to tell us she had taken a large dose of opium with suicidal intent. My assistant hurried to her home, five miles away, to administer remedies to save her if he could. But she was beyond the aid of mortal — the spirit had departed.

This woman was twenty-eight years old — attractive and intelligent. Her husband had been dead eight years. He was sixty she fifteen when they were married. For five years she roasted his opium and held his pipe — a slave rather than a wife. That she should have acquired a taste for the drug is but natural. For nine years she used it regularly. The family heard of our ability to free

opium slaves and she came to
us gladly. She heard the gospel daily — how much she understood and accepted we can never
know. Let the assistant speak.
"She returned to her home strong —
the longing for opium was all
gone. All the family were pleased
with her. Two weeks after she
returned her husbands brother
announced that he had sold her
to a rich man in the city. This
man had four or five wives
but they all took opium and he
needed some one to wait on him.
The poor woman said she would
not go. She had served one man
and had been a slave for thirteen
years. She was a slave no longer and she would remain free.
The man tried to force her to do
his bidding and at last she
told him she would die first.
The woman told them it was not
right for the old man to have so
many wives — the True God said so.

A Slave No Longer

Today she was to go to her slavery again, but she went to her death instead."

Poor woman! She preferred death to such a life. She did not know enough of the True God to keep her from taking her life. She had a taste of something better, she had a little Light and she followed the Light as far as she knew. Her death will pass unnoticed. There will be one mouth less for her husbands brother to feed. Had she lived and refused to obey the man's order her life would have been one continuous round of abuse and she would have been subject to many wrongs and contumelies. Had she entered the rich man's home she would soon have been a slave, a double slave, again. Did she choose the better portion?

Yours Very Truly.
W. L. Hall.

Chapter 10 -
Marriage Arrangement & Homemade Shoes

Letter No. 9.

Liman, Shansi, China.

April 1897.

"Doctor, I have heard that in your country the men ask the women to marry them. Is it true or not?"

I was surprised at the tone of the speaker. We were not discussing that subject and as the man turned to me in such a simple child-like way I felt that his question did not show mere curiosity. "That is our usual custom." "Did you say to Mrs Hall 'will you marry me?' and did she reply 'yes, Dr. Hall, I will'? and were you all alone? and did you drink tea together before you asked her? and did your "middle-man" hear you ask her and hear her answer?" I answered the last question by saying "we do not require a middle-man in America." "But who guarantees your wife if you do not have a middleman? how do you know what she can do? did you see any of her work before you asked her? could

Marriage Arrangement & Homemade Shoes

she do her food and sew and make
shoes? how did you know she did
not take opium? ("but you are a
doctor you could tell that yourself.)"
"I had eaten food prepared by her,
I knew she could sew, but I did
not once think of asking her if
she could make shoes" "Could
she make shoes?"!! I will
say here by way of explanation
that "making shoes" should be
called "the old Man of the Sea" to
chinese women. Wherever and wherever you go you will see young
women and old stitch! stitch!
stitch!-ing away — making shoes.
From childhood to dotage the
weary round goes on. In season
and out of season may be seen
the moving thread, thro and thro,
back and forth, with incessant
and unvaried monotony. Her own
tiny shoes must be made at spare
moments and in the secrecy of her
own room. But the husband and
the father and the sons so must

Marriage Arrangement & Homemade Shoes

have shoes and the women must
have them ready when called for.
If more shoes can be made than
present necessity requires the shops
will take them to sell to their
customers. All common shoes
are made of cloth — tops, sides
soles and all. Not a scrap of
cloth lent can be utilized. The
sides of the shoes are usually of
new cloth — may be cheapest blue
cloth or finest velvet, — but any thing
will do for the insides of the
thick soles. These are made by
pasting together several thicknesses of material, the outside
is covered with new cloth and the
whole mass is then sewed together.
The soles may be from one-fourth
inch to two inches thick and
the shoes — as I find them — are
most uncomfortable. The toes
are pressed together and the heel slips
up and down in a most provok-
ing manner. I think, sometimes,
the chinese would be more en-

Marriage Arrangement & Homemade Shoes

terprising in a different foot-gear.
I know I would.
But I turned the tables.
I said, "Mr. Wang, did you ask
your wife to marry you?"
"Me? No! She had nothing to do
with it. All she had to do was
to get married." "How long did
you know your wife before you
were married?" "What do you
mean? How long did I know my
wife before we were married?
I did not know her at all.
Why should I trouble myself
about that? The affair was
managed by the middleman.
I was at home at my work. You
see I did not have so much
bother to get my wife as you
did to get yours." "How did
you manage the affair to get
your wife?" Did I not tell
you that I did not manage the
affair? I engaged the middleman to find me a wife and told
him how much I could spend for

Marriage Arrangement & Homemade Shoes

a wife and — "Oh, I see. You told the middleman what kind of a wife you wanted; that she must be such — and — such an age, and clever and — " "No! of course I did not! If I should do all this what need would I have for a middleman? I told him I wanted a wife; it was his affair to find her." "How did he manage to find her?" "I do not know. He found her and I had no cause to ask questions." "But I want to know how he found her." "Why? do you want another wife?" "No! I want to know your custom, that is all." "I do not know the custom in other villages but the middleman must announce that he wants a wife for such-and-such a man; she must be able to work, must be born on a lucky day, must be good-looking and must be able to show some of her work. She must be of a

Marriage Arrangement & Homemade Shoes

different family — (i.e. Wang cannot marry Wang, Wu cannot
marry Wu, Han cannot marry
Han, etc W.H.) and must furnish
her own bedding." "Did you
see her before you were married?" "Yes, I saw her once, after the affair was settled.
"Did you discuss the matter?"
"No, I did not speak to her, That
would have been most indelicate."

It is said that nothing
can dissolve a contract after it
is completed. The girl knows
nothing of the man she is to
marry. I know a case — have
seen the man many times
and the girl belonged to this village. She was engaged to him,
he was wealthy and paid more
for her than any of the other
applicants. One who knew the
girl says she was a beautiful
girl — pleasant and industrious.
The family were in easy circum-

Chapter 10 -
And Death Is Powerless

stances, but the girl was always
at her work. She had nothing
to say about the plan for her
future. She was not permitted to speak to her intended
husband before marriage — and
she could not after the ceremony.
Not until after she was taken
to his home did she know that
her husband was a mute.
He was deaf and dumb — had
never heard a sound or spok-
en a word in his life. The
girl died last June — but not until
she had borne four children
to her husband — the two older
like the father, the third like her
self — the baby four days old when
the cord of life was broken and
a life of untold misery and
sadness was at an end forever.

And Death itself is power-
less to release a girl from
her bonds — if Death choose to
take the man for whom she

And Death Is Powerless

is intended. Two years ago, in this village, a man died a short time before the date set for the marriage ceremony. Did his death release the girl? No! at the appointed time she was united to his spirit and is now his widow. A dummy, or image, was used to represent the man — this image was carried in the chair in the wedding procession that the dead man would have occupied had he been living. The girl followed after, in her chair, and arrayed in the garments of a bride. Some part of the ceremony was at the grave — she was united to each of his three spirits (or souls) and must go through life as with this relationship. I have not heard a more pathetic story.

We came to China to tell the people of a Way, a Truth and a Life — that Way will change

And Death Is Powerless

the lot of these poor women when
china is brought to the Truth and
the Life.   I find so much
sadness in the lives of these women. They are only women and
being women they can only accept a woman's portion.
        Born to lives of sadness and
misery and physical suffering,
having no pleasure in this life
or hope for the life to come, it
does not surprise one when they
find oblivion through opium.
I asked one poor, pitiful woman why she did not let her
baby daughter live. She replied
"I could not let it live for even
two days when I knew what was
before it if its lot in life was
as its mother's." —
        We have now, more than thir-
ty women in the hospital, I see
them and hear their stories of suffering and loneliness and hopeless-
less every day.   Pain, pain,
pain! here, there and everywhere

And Death Is Powerless

Their lot in life most sad; their lives so dreary and monotonous! Two have not walked for years. They sit from day to day, with folded hands and saddened faces, looking forward to death and — what? We have no one (foreigner) to speak to them. Mrs. Hall goes to them every Sunday and every second day during the week. She is doing all she can for them, but her family requires much at her hands. If could you see the happy faces, made so by a kind word, a flower or a bit of dainty food you would not need to be told why Mrs. Hall is so happy in China or why God has blessed us both by bringing us to this place.

We pray daily for more help for these women and we will pray on, until help comes. May the dear Lord send some one from our own church, or state or coast to do for these "the least" of His children.

Yours very truly,

W. L. Hall.

PATRICIA BAILEY

Patricia Bailey was born in Huron, South Dakota, raised in Denver, Colorado and has spent most of her adult life in Washington State and Arizona. Along with her sister, Susan, she spent a year living abroad and traveling extensively throughout Europe. Living there was the beginning of her love of art, portrait painting, architecture and design.

At 21 years of age, she married Architect Garrison Bailey. They worked together for many years at his architectural firm in Phoenix, Arizona. After acquiring Dr. Hall's residence, they moved to Washington State and worked at various architecture firms. Both shared a passion for juicing and nutrition and opened a chain of juice bars.

Patricia became a licensed real estate broker in 2003 and retains a broker's license in Arizona.

Throughout most of her adult life, Patricia has been a portrait painter, avid reader and loves to hike and play golf. All of which she now enjoys living in Scottsdale, Arizona and Tubac, Arizona.

It was always her goal to have Dr. Hall's journals published to honor his amazing life and is grateful to see this become a reality.